The ZORN Conspiracy

by

Edward E. Peoples

10 9 8 7 6 5 4 3 2 1 - Meadow Crest Publishing Company

This book is dedicated to Hatfield,
my guide and mentor in life,
for his ready wisdom and counsel.

Chapter 1

The motel radio alarm came on at 6:30 a.m., blaring out a local traffic report: *stop and go traffic over the Golden Gate Bridge. Two lanes on the lower deck of the Bay Bridge closed because of a four car accident.* I shut off the radio and sat for a moment on the edge of the bed, getting my bearings and shaking the cobwebs out of my head.

I had checked in to the room last night about 8:00 pm, *let me think. OK, now I remember why I'm here.* I got up and set the motel room's Mr. Coffee to drip, then went into the small bathroom to complete my morning's shave and shower routine. It was 7:05 a.m. when I stepped out of the shower, dried, and slipped on a clean pair of shorts. I'd been asked to arrive at room 14 at 9:00 a.m. sharp. A matter of urgent state business and of the utmost secrecy, the caller had said. He had identified himself as Carl Jessup, special assistant to State Attorney General Ronald Colton.

I promised to meet him. However, my suspicious nature prompted me to check into the motel the evening before so that I might learn something about what I was getting into before I did. In retrospect, that was probably unnecessary. The motel was located in the south end of San Rafael, just off the 101 freeway and about twenty minutes north of San Francisco. I had purposefully booked a room on the second floor directly across the parking area from room 14.

Looking out my window last night, I could see that the large blue and pink neon sign of the motel, *The Dunes*, was still blinking on and off, but several bulbs had burned out over the years, so those remaining spelled *Th D nes* when lit. During the 1950s, '60s, and even the '70s, so I was told, the motel boasted a dining room and large bar, with pianist/vocalist Sage Costa, and had been the favorite watering hole, dining sight, and tryst spot for the wealthy locals. However, in recent years the lounge and big-band ball room had been cut up into small, cheap apartments, and many of the once plush motel rooms now featured mirrored ceilings and adult videos. I imagine one could get hourly rates as well.

My small room contained a double bed with a blond bookcase headboard, matching end tables, a desk with a maple-stained wooden chair, and a large over-stuffed chair with green frieze upholstery. A small Mr. Coffee pot, plastic ice bucket, and two plastic glasses rested in a tray on the desk. The beige carpet was stained and worn, and the green and floral print drapes were thread bare.

I had slept off and on during the night in the overstuffed chair, which I had pulled next to the window so I could see if anyone else came in and occupied any of the other rooms. I think I was right about the hourly rates; because over the next six hours I had observed twenty-seven cars drive in, then leave after about an hour or two.

One of the cars had been a taxi that stopped in front of room 14 about 1:30 a.m. A dark haired female dressed in light blue running pants and top got out of the taxi. The room door opened, and she was quickly ushered into the room. The taxi waited there for about forty minutes, and then she came out of the room, jumped into the back seat, and the cab quietly left. Must have been a hefty tab to pay for the man in room 14.

Only three cars remained parked in front of the rooms in the morning. The one in front of room 14 was a 2007 metallic green Ford 4-door sedan with blackwall tires and no chrome.

At 8:15 a.m., a 2008 gray Chevrolet Impala coupe drove in and parked next to the Ford. The driver scanned the area slowly, then got out and approached room 14. He was a short squatty man in his mid-50s, with broad shoulders, thick jowls, and short-cropped silver gray hair. The room door opened before he could knock. He gave a quick glance to each side, and then darted into the room.

A second car drove in almost immediately and parked. Two men in the front seat looked around the parking lot, then emerged from the car and walked directly to room 14. One man was a tall blond, dressed in a three-piece gray pin-striped suit, white shirt and a red paisley tie. Each hair was neatly styled into place, and the toes of his shoes glistened in the morning sun. The second man was dark skinned, Mexican perhaps, with long dark curly hair that bounced in all directions as he walked. He wore green slacks and a black and white checkered sport coat, both of which looked as if they'd been slept in. They entered room 14 as quickly as the first men had.

A third and fourth car drove in almost simultaneously. The drivers surveyed the motel grounds, then looked at each other and nodded. They exited their vehicles, checked the area again, and then walked quickly to room 14. They were dressed like businessmen attending a board meeting, neatly attired in dark brown suits, well groomed, and precise in their movements.

I watched until 8:30 to see if any other cars would arrive. In the meantime, I gulped the bitter coffee, washing down two pieces of cold ham and pineapple pizza left over from the night before. That, along with a half pint of *Jose Cuervo Gold,* had been my dinner.

It was 8:45. Almost time to make my grand entrance. I put on my faded Levis and pulled on my old, but comfortable harness boots, and finished dressing between gulps of coffee. The pizza was tough and chewy, but it absorbed the bitter coffee and filled in the hollow spot in my stomach.

I didn't know what I was getting into, so just in case this was some sort of setup, I shoved my Colt Mustang .380 down inside my boot, threw my dirty socks and shorts into a bag that I brought, locked the door and walked down the stairs. I put the bag in my car, and then went to the motel office to check out before making my appointed visit to room 14.

A dull buzzer sounded as I opened the office door. A scrawny looking man in his mid-20s was sitting behind the counter. He put down a magazine he had been reading, or looking at, and watched me approach, waiting for me to offer the first word.

"I checking out," I said.

"Which room?" His tone was matter-of-fact, but not unfriendly.

"39. Here's the key." I read the name tag pinned to his faded but ironed shirt: *Larry*.

"OK, you're all set."

"Say Larry, were you on duty all night," I asked, trying to sound interested.

"Yep, from 9:00 p.m. 'til 9:30 a.m. this morning." Then he did a sort of double-take and said, "Do I know you?"

"I don't think so. Why do you ask?"

"You called me by name." His voice raised in a questioning tone.

"Oh, I just read your name on your tag there. Long shift, huh?" I said, again trying to sound interested. He seemed satisfied.

"Sure is, but I like it. Quiet. No bosses around and no one to hassle me, and the boss says I can study when we're not busy. I'm going to the local community college."

"I'll bet you are, Larry. Did you notice the taxi that pulled in here about 1:30 a.m. this morning and left after about forty minutes? A girl got out and went into room 14."

"I'm sorry sir I don't make it my business to know who stays here or why," he responded with a bland, but humble tone. His dull brown eyes had a blank expression, if that's possible. "Will that be all, sir?"

I pulled a $20.00 bill out of my wallet and waved it toward him. "Are you sure you don't know anything about the party in room 14?"

"Well, I'll tell you what. We follow that old military motto, *don't ask, don't tell*. We survive here only because we know that privacy is our most important product, or service, in this case. I wouldn't tell you who came to room 14 any more than I would tell the guy who asked who stayed in room 39 last night! Get my meaning?"

"I see your point, Larry. I congratulate you on your style of honor, I think." I shrugged and put away the $20.

Chapter 2

I left the motel office and walked across the asphalt parking area toward room 14. I saw the curtain move slightly as I approached, and the door opened before I could knock.

"Come in Dr. Worth." The voice was low and steady, but the tone seemed friendly.

I entered and quickly scanned the room and observed that it was larger than mine, with two double beds, walnut-stained furniture, pale yellow frieze coverings on the chairs, yellow and floral print drapes, and yellow bed spreads. The furniture was equally as old as that in my room, but the carpet was new. There was a small kitchen area with an efficiency and sink separated from the bedroom by a narrow Formica-topped counter. This must have been one of those suites that they rented on a monthly basis.

The man with the low voice shut the door as soon as I was in the room. "Good morning, Dr. Worth. I'm Wayne Jessup, Special Assistant to Ronald Colton, State's Attorney General. I'm the one who asked you to meet with us."

He was short, about 5' 6", and sixty pounds overweight, with a fringe of stringy brown hair that he combed over the balding portion of his head. He had a pinkish fleshy face and pale green eyes. I could see why he might have had to pay for female favors, but at the same time I sympathized with how she must have felt having to service him.

"Mr. Jessup." I shook his hand, and then looked at the other men around the room. The two business-types who had arrived last were seated next to a round Formica top table at the opposite end of the room, sipping coffee.

The short squatty man was leaning against the bar counter separating the living portion from the kitchen, holding a freshly opened can of Coors beer. The dark, curly haired man was sprawled upright on one of the beds with his shoes off, watching television with the sound turned off. A sixth man, whom I hadn't seen enter the room, was standing near the sliding door that opened to the rear of the motel area. His legs were spread apart, his arms were folded across his flat stomach, and he was staring at me intently.

Jessup made the introductions. "This is Ray Garcia," pointing to the man sprawled on the bed. "He's with the Federal Drug Enforcement Administration." I nodded, and he waved one hand without lifting his arm. I expected to see cartoons on the TV, but it was a morning talk show.

"This is Philip Holden," Jessup continued, gesturing toward the tall, neatly groomed man in the three-piece suit standing near the sliding rear door. "He's an Assistant United States Attorney." Jessup articulated the words quickly and very clearly, as if he knew that one of his ilk was very concerned about being titled correctly. We exchanged nods.

Jessup continued, "The two gentlemen seated at the table are Rex Jamison, Special Agent with the FBI, and Robert Orneles, investigator for the State Department of Justice. He works directly out of Attorney General Colton's office." Both nodded and offered canned smiles. "And, last but not least, is Bill MacClanahan, Mac we call him," he said, pointing to the man holding the beer. "He's a special investigator for the State Department of Corrections and Rehabilitation."

The man with the short-cropped hair was not as short as he first appeared when he had exited his car. He was barrel-chested, with broad shoulders, a whiskey-reddened face with voice to match, and a piercing look in his steel-blue eyes. What classic features. He had the weathered look of an old harness bull who had worked the cell blocks as a guard for years, doing life on the installment plan. His face broke into a warm smile and he stepped forward to grasp my hand in a quick but firm shake, and then retreated to his post at the counter.

"Gentlemen," Jessup continued. "May I present Dr. Matthew Z. Worth."

There was a moment of silence as they all looked at me. Orneles, from the AG's office, had maintained his intense stare since I walked into the room. Now, his eyes scanned me up and down with an air of disapproval. I had deliberately dressed for the occasion in my faded Levis, sweat shirt, and harness boots. I grinned at him, and then looked back at Jessup.

"Well, Dr. Worth, that's quite a handle," Jessup commented, referring to my full name, "but I imagine you are wondering what this is all about."

"The thought was just starting across my mind," I said, "but first, gentlemen, let me say that whatever it is, I didn't do it and I'll never do it again." The old bull, MacClanahan, was the only one who smiled. I got the distinct feeling that we were not here to exchange pleasantries.

"Sit down, Dr. Worth, please," offered Jessup, looking quickly around the small room for an empty chair.

"That's all right," I said. "I might as well be as comfortable as Garcia there, and I crossed the room and took up a position near the second bed, fluffed up two pillows and arranged them as a back rest, then laid back, grinned at Garcia, and surveyed the other men.

"May I offer you refreshments, Dr. Worth," said Jessup. "Some coffee? Juice? or..."

"Yes, thanks," I interrupted. "I'll join MacClanahan, there, in a beer"

MacClanahan took a fresh Coors from the refrigerator, handed it to Jessup who handed it to me. He must have brought a six-pack for himself. I popped the lid and drew deeply.

"Gentlemen, I'm all ears. Why am I here?" I deliberately changed my tone mid-sentence from casual to one more demanding.

"Yes, Dr. Worth," blurted Jessup. "Of course. Let's get on with it." He sat gingerly on one corner of the bed. "We asked you here to help us solve a problem, to help us stop the spread of a serious criminal threat in our state; to offer you an unique job opportunity."

"I have a job," I responded.

"Yes, I know." Jessup was patient, almost condescending. "Please, hear us out. MacClanahan, perhaps you would begin?"

MacClanahan took a final pull on his beer, threw the empty can in the basket, and popped open a fresh Coors from the refrigerator. "Here's the situation, Worth. Our prisons are busting at the seams. We got inmates stacked like cord wood, and more coming in every day. We're even resorting to erecting tents and putting 3-tiered cots in the gyms at several prisons. The stupid legislature passed that determinate sentencing law way back in 1977, without considering the consequences, like it usually does, and it's been toughening up the criminal penalties every year since, without providing money to expand the prison system fast enough to keep pace. The public voted 'no' on the last two prison bond issues, and the State is nearly broke."

"I'm familiar with the problem, MacClanahan." I interjected, "but I thought that the legislature was considering allocating funds to build six new prisons. Also, I understood that the governor was planning to transfer thousands of inmates to prisons out of state on a contract basis, and releasing many on early parole."

"A drop in the bucket, my boy, a drop in the bucket," responded MacClanahan. "Our population is over 180,000 now, and even if we could open those six prisons, which is not very likely, given the current budget problems, we'd still be about 95,000 over capacity, and the correctional officers union is pressuring the governor to drop the transfer plan. I know you're familiar with some of our problems, Worth, because of your studies. Then you know we've been plagued with prison gang violence for years. The blacks and whites have been killing each other, and the two Mexican gangs have been at war, killing each other both in and out of prison."

"Yes, I am aware of all that. It all started years ago in Folsom Prison over the ownership of a pair of shoes." MacClanahan looked surprised at my remark, as if such knowledge was reserved only for insiders.

"Well, most of the violence now has been over who would control the prison population and drug traffic. We didn't mind as long as they were killing each other inside. That kept them off our back, but when they extended their violence and control into the streets, we got concerned. That's when I moved into intelligence. I've been tracking the gang members on parole for the last eighteen years, and we have been able to control them, or at least know who was doing what. That is until last March, three months ago. All of a sudden things got quiet. The violence stopped inside. Then we noticed that the gang leaders were meeting together."

"Meeting?" I asked. "What do you mean, meeting? How could they meet? I thought you kept them spread around the different prisons?"

"Lawyers," MacClanahan replied. "Most of the gang members are represented by ALF, the American Lawyers Federation, a bunch of pinko commie queers who'd like nothing better than to see our whole prison system erupt in one gigantic people's revolution. They get them together by subpoenas under some due process gimmick, and then let them plan what they want, for a price, of course. We think that out of those meetings has come a new organization. A new gang, if you will, formed by the top leaders. We think they have called a truce among themselves to unite in a new scheme. We've intercepted certain letters and have received rumors from a couple of informants. But we don't know exactly what they're up to. The word ZORN has been referred to in some of the letters, but we don't know what that means. However, we do have an idea of what their goal is."

"I'm listening, Mac," I said, trying to change the nature of the conversation to one with more personal rapport. "But I'm not connecting any of this with me." I was pleasant with MacClanahan because he had none of the usual bureaucratic pretenses and he was personable toward me.

"Perhaps this will make the connection for you. Two months ago the state of California received a $37.2 billion federal grant to establish a network of community correctional centers throughout the state. Prison bailout money, as it were. Since we have no more room beyond the walls, we are going to set up a number of these centers, and fill them with low risk offenders, who can benefit more from community treatment than the traditional lock-up. There is also a plan to make these centers joint county-state lockups, where they'll include jail inmates serving a year and prison inmates serving three years or less, and managed by private corporations. Half way in and half way out."

"Low risk offenders," I interjected. "I didn't think you had any more low risk types in prison. I thought only the violent and hard core offenders went to prison today."

"Well," responded Jessup. "In a sense you're right. However, we are going to *push up the risk factor*, as they say. We have no other choice. And, the community will be safe, too. Rest assured."

He was not too convincing with his last offering. His thinking was typical of the way those in government make policy decisions without ever asking the governed.

"We don't have the manpower," Jessup continued, "nor the expertise to establish, staff, and administer the correctional centers ourselves. Consequently, we are going to contract with other public and selected private organizations or individuals to do it for us. We think that will be more cost-effective and result in more community involvement. It will be California's grand experiment in privatized community corrections."

"I read something about this in a press release that Governor Colton issued last month. It stated that the State Board of Corrections would administer the overall program and distribute the individual grants. I also heard from some colleagues that Dick James was hired as a corrections consultant to screen the applicants and work directly with the grant recipients to facilitate the creation of the various centers. He's a good man. I know of your program, gentlemen, and I still don't know why I'm here, and I'm beginning to resent the stall." I started to get off the bed as if to leave.

MacClanahan stepped forward. "You see, Worth, we think that somehow these prison gang leaders got wind of this program and are going to try to get their hands on all that money. We aren't certain, but we believe that the gang leaders have worked out this truce and joined forces to gain control over the correctional centers. And, we don't know who else might be involved."

"How can they have access to the grant money if they're locked up in prison?"

"That's the problem, Worth. Many of the leaders are out on parole now, and those inside still have control over the membership. At this point, the information we have is too sketchy. There are a number of legitimate applicants for the grants, but there might be some gang related organizations as well. Right now we can't tell the good guys from the bad guys. We need someone on the inside, someone we can trust."

I stood, facing MacClanahan. "I don't like what I think you're leading up to. I'm no informant or undercover man. And, besides, you can trust Dick James all the way."

This was beginning to sound like a long-term and involved deal they were trying to suck me into, and I was becoming gun-shy of their sort of approach. Actually, I had been looking forward to having the summer free from teaching, and I thought if I sounded indignant enough, it could get me out of their seemingly good graces. I started to rise from the bed.

"James is dead," MacClanahan responded in a low whiskey-voiced whisper. "He died last week in his Sacramento apartment. Electrocuted himself when he stuck a butter knife in the toaster, the coroner said."

"My God. I didn't read... I didn't hear." I was stunned. I sat back down on the bed. I knew Dick James by professional reputation and I respected him as a colleague. Why hadn't I read about his death in the paper? Before I could regain my composure, Jessup spoke.

"What we want, Dr. Worth," offered Jessup, "is someone who knows the system and who has the integrity we can trust to work with us. We want you to replace James. You'll review the grant applications, make cursory investigations of the applicants, check out their proposed facilities, recommend who should receive the funds, and nose around and decide who we should monitor for possible criminal involvement."

"Cursory investigations? What do you mean by cursory?" I queried.

Rex Jamison unfolded his arms and took two strides toward the bed. "That means that you'll do routine interviews and background checks on the applicants, inspect their proposed facility and staff, and then inform us about what you've learned. We'll follow up on anyone you think looks *hinky*. We'll handle the heavy stuff."

"How far do I go in my cursory investigations? That is, what's the area of my jurisdiction, as it were?" I asked.

The Los Angeles, Orange, and San Diego County sheriff's departments will receive approximately half the grant money to establish seven residential centers in southern California. Those will combine both county jail inmates and state parolees. We call it a half-way in/half-way out approach. Your work will focus on the area from Bakersfield north. That is where the experiment in privatization will be centered. All we want you to do beyond what I've stated is to mix and develop open relationships with everyone you can. Hopefully, you'll be able to shake something out of this for us. We don't anticipate any trouble for you, no danger, if that is what concerns you."

"Open relationships and cursory investigations, you say. No danger, huh? Then why do I get the feeling that I'm going to need a douche when I leave here?"

"Dr. Worth," began Jessup. "I can assure you..."

I interrupted. "Is that what you told James? Did you assure Dick James there was no danger?"

"Look Dr. Worth!" It was Jamison of the FBI speaking in a staccato voice and looking at Jessup, while he addressed me. "James was electrocuted; a stupid accident. He wasn't there long enough to learn anything useful. If it turns out to be more than that, we'll let you know immediately."

I didn't feel reassured. Their approach was like the proverbial iceberg. They show me the tip and hope I don't run into the body below and sink. "If all you need is a knowledgeable and trusted consultant, why me? Why not some low-level bureaucrat already supping at the public trough? And why does it take heavies like you from so many agencies to work this thing?"

"One question at a time, Dr. Worth." Jessup was standing now, walking around the room waving his arms, trying to orchestrate his thoughts. "Although we don't know who is involved yet, we do think it is a big operation. As I said, what we think might be a code word, ZORN, keeps popping up in certain gang correspondence. There may even be a link between the prison gangs and organized crime. We know the gangs are heavily into the drug distribution in California, and may use the centers as fronts to increase their operations. The gang leaders might siphon some of the grant money into their personal accounts or into other businesses. It might also be used to support certain political candidates. We just want to cover all the bases. Ideally, we want to nail them on federal drug charges. Or, better yet, on the federal RICO statute, racketeering influence in corrupting organizations. We want to put them in federal prison where we know they will do long, hard time."

"Okay, Jessup. I'll buy that." I really didn't. They were still covering something. "But why me? What do you know about me that makes you think I'm your man?"

"Mr. Orneles," responded Jessup, nodding to the state investigator from DOJ, who had been glaring at me the entire time. "Will you summarize Dr. Worth's file for us please."

Orneles smirked, privately lauding his clever possession of certain knowledge. He was on stage. He picked up a folder from the table, skimmed it momentarily, stood up, and then began reading from the dossier he had compiled on me. "Matthew Z. Worth: born July 13, 1978 in the small mining town of Gabbs, Nevada, the youngest of three children raised by his natural parents, William and Janice Worth, both deceased."

Jessup interrupted, "The short version Orneles, just give us the short version."

Orneles seemed put off by Jessup's urge to hurry and get this all over with. "O.K., Mr. Jessup. Just the facts, as they say. Graduated from Ely High School, graduated from the University of Nevada, Reno in 2002, with a BA, and then a Master's degree in criminal justice in 2005. While going to college, worked three years as a police officer for Reno PD, and two years as a county probation officer. Completed his doctorate at UNR in 2008. Married Libby Marie Stone in March 2006. Separated off and on for several years, and then divorced in 2009. Drives a 2008 gray Chevy king-cab pickup. Has worked the last three years as a part-time lecturer in various criminal justice courses for three different community colleges in the Bay Area. Refused a tenured track assistant professor position at San Jose State University. Considered by some to be bright and dedicated to students. Considered by others to be an irresponsible maverick and rebel who won't join the academic fraternity and fulfill his potential. Also licensed by the state as a private investigator, and pursues that occupation from time to time. Off work now from the colleges for summer vacation.

"Not bad, Orneles, not bad at all," I said, not bothering to hide the irritation in my voice. I have a disdain for bureaucratic snoops and government agents. "But, you forgot my height, 6′ 2″ (standing tall, with my harness boots on), weight 195 pounds, sandy blond hair, gray-blue eyes, and blood type B negative."

"By the way, Dr. Worth," Orneles responded, "what's the middle initial Z stand for?"

"It stands for Zeno, an old family name. Do you want my complete family tree as well?"

"No need to get upset, Dr. Worth," said Jessup. "We just wanted you to know that we've considered you very carefully. You have the academic credentials and respect of your peers. No one will question your appointment to the job. You have the integrity and enforcement background to do us some good, and you like the independence this job can offer. You're our man."

He was sounding more convincing, and I was just blowing smoke anyway. I relaxed and sat down on the bed.

"Well, Dr. Worth, what about it? Will you help us? We need you. And you will be helping your country as well." Jessup was being as nice as anyone could and he was almost pleading.

"How much does the job pay?" I asked.

"$67,000 per year, plus a car allowance and any direct expenses."

"How long do you think it will take me to uncover what you need?" I asked.

"Hard to say." Jessup tried to look thoughtful. "Two, maybe three months."

"What happens to the job then?" I asked.

"Well..."Jessup hesitated. "I suppose you could stay on as a program consultant, but... I... we...we expected that you would want out as soon as your role was finished, but..."

"I would, but that means the pay checks will be short lived. Here's the deal. I'll consider it, but I want the entire year's salary up front. The full $67,000 in the bank when I start, plus $300 a month to cover all expenses as long as the job lasts." I thought I might as well push a little. I thought I was in a good bargaining position because they wanted me and I didn't want them.

Jessup looked at Holden, who gave a quick nod of ascent. "Very well, Dr. Worth, it's yours."

"When do I begin?"

"This is Thursday. You may start Monday. The grant project is handled out of the State Board of Corrections office. I assume that you know where they are located, and the director is expecting you Monday morning. That will give you three days to get settled in Sacramento. Here are the keys to your apartment. It's located on Cabrillo Court, a nice quiet area within easy walking distance from downtown and Old Town. Here's a Google map, with directions."

"My apartment?"

"Well, actually, it's the apartment we rented for Dick James. We have a year's lease. But, his things are all moved out. It's furnished, but you may personalize it however you like. The rent is $1,425 a month and we've already paid through August. Here is the address and the key to your office at the Board of Corrections.

I had that sucked-in feeling again. "Tell me, Mr. Jessup, what if I didn't take the job?" I was just curious to see if they thought of that as a possibility.

"We would tell you that we would offer it to Robert Tyler at UC Santa Cruz."

"Tyler, why that fraud. He's a disgrace to his profession. He's...."

"Exactly, Dr. Worth." Jessup smiled to let me know he'd won again. You see, we know your dislikes, as well. We also know that you are two months behind on your truck payment, and owe a considerable amount on two Visa bills."

I was beginning to think they knew more about me than I did, and that bothered me. I consider myself to be a very private person with a strong need to control every aspect of my life. I wanted to keep it that way. However, he was right about the current state of my finances. "Who's my contact?"

"Garcia here is one. In fact he has applied for one of the corrections grants that you'll be reviewing, and has tentative approval to begin preparing a location, pending final review and approval. We want you to see that he is approved and awarded some of the funds. He's been working undercover for three years in Florida, so he is not known out here. He will set up a center in North Sacramento for two hundred inmates, who will be transferred from Folsom Prison. It will seem natural for you to stop by and check on his operation from time to time."

"He'll be reporting directly to Holden, who is coordinating the task force. MacClanahan will also be in contact with you on a regular basis. And if you want to check out the possible gang affiliation of anyone, you can contact him. He knows them all."

"O.K., you have a deal. However, before I leave I want the phone numbers where I can reach each at you day or night. No offense." I looked over to Garcia. He grinned and turned back to the television. Each of them pulled a business card out of their wallet and started to hand them to me. "Wait a minute, gentlemen. I want phone numbers where I can reach any of you at any time, 24 hours a day."

They all looked to Holden who nodded, then they penned in phone numbers and handed me the cards.

"Anything else?" Jessup asked.

"Yes. Who else knows about this operation? I don't like surprises."

"The heads of each of our agencies, no one else. We haven't even told the Governor. Colton wanted to keep the State's role coming exclusively out of his office."

"No one else?" I asked.

"No one," assured Jessup.

"O.K., gentlemen. I'm in," I said in my most pleasant tone. They all nodded approval at each other, then left one-by-one just as they had arrived. Only MacClanahan took the trouble to shake my hand again and offer me his personal approval. I turned to leave, and Jessup accompanied me to the door. I took the soft fleshy hand he offered. It did not squeeze; it just laid there in mine. I looked down expecting to see a little fish eye looking up at me.

"Well, Dr. Worth, it's a pleasure having you with us. I can't impress you strongly enough about the importance of your efforts, and of the secrecy of this operation. Any information, no matter how trivial, pass it on. We'll all stay in touch."

"I'm good at gathering information," I said. "And speaking of secrecy, how much did you tell that little whore you had in here last night?"

"What whore...? " he stammered. "Why I don't… ."

"Yes, you do." I stood close and tried to stare him down. "That little hooker you had in here screwing until 2:00 a.m. this morning. How much did you let slip to her?"

He shuddered and his pinkish face turned pale. "Nothing. I told her nothing. We just..."

"Good. Remember, I don't like surprises." I was beginning not to like Jessup much either. He was a yes-man, without any real commitment outside of himself.

Chapter 3

As I approached my pickup, I looked over and spotted MacClanahan pumping gas into his car at the station across from the motel. That gave me an idea. The card he had given me had no address, only a phone number. If he was going to be one of my contacts, it might be useful to know where he works; assuming he was going back to work. I reached my pickup just in time to see him pull away from the pumps. His car would be easy enough to recognize and follow: a Ford with no chrome, blackwall tires, and a short antenna protruding out of the trunk lid.

I drove out of the motel and watched MacClanahan take the 101 freeway on-ramp heading toward San Francisco. I didn't want to get too close because my pickup truck might be easy for him to spot, so I stayed six to eight car lengths behind him. As we drove down the approach to the Golden Gate Bridge, I watched the summer fog creeping back out to sea, leaving swirls of thick mist that shrouded the bridge towers.

A number of tourists were already gathering at Vista Point or were walking across the bridge, all with cameras or camcorders hanging from their shoulders. We drove over the bridge, through the toll gate, and bore left toward the water-front, past the Marina and Fisherman's Wharf, then along the docks. Suddenly, without any signal, he turned left and disappeared into one of the old empty pier warehouses that lined the waterfront; one of those that had not as yet experienced the City's efforts at remodeling.

I parked about three piers down, in a grass covered lot across the street, and waited. There was no sign of life. After about ten minutes, I left my car and walked quickly across the street and back to the corner of the warehouse that MacClanahan had entered. There once were rows of pier warehouses separated by slips where ships from all over the world used to dock and unload their cargos. Most of them had been empty now for many years, ever since one of the local politicos destroyed the City's shipping business in an organized crime conspiracy, just to pad his own pocket. At least that is the story that my friend Hatfield told me.

Hatfield always said that if you make a politician out of a lawyer, you get it in the end with both barrels.

I walked quietly down the old wooden dock alongside the warehouse, hoping to find a window or knothole through which I could observe inside. I wished now that I had changed my boots for sneakers; they would have given me a better sense of sneaking. Ahead was a large open door where the forklifts used to dart in and out conveying their pallet loads of cargo to or from the waiting ship. I approached it cautiously and listened. Nothing. I took a chance and poked my head around the corner and into the warehouse. Stacks of empty pallets were still piled here and there. Thick cobwebs hung from the high ceiling. There was no sign of life.

Suddenly, I heard voices echoing down from the street end of the warehouse. I moved inside, behind a stack of pallets, and peered over the top. MacClanahan's car was parked next to a small glassed-in office. A single shaded light hung from the ceiling. The light was dim, but I could see MacClanahan's large frame seated, tilting in a chair next to a small desk. Four men stood in a semi-circle facing him. *What's he up to?* I wondered. If I could just get a little closer.

I ducked around the other side of the pallets and made my way forward, weaving in and out of the other stacks of pallets that were piled at random down the side of the warehouse. I was close now. The voices were loud, but the words were only a series of blurred inflections. I found a pallet with the open end facing toward the office and peered through it. Three black men and a Mexican man stood facing MacClanahan, their legs apart, arms folded in front, and their bodies erect. The blacks were dressed in old jeans and army fatigue jackets. One wore a patch over one eye. The other two wore red bandanas on their heads. One was tall and gaunt, and wore studded earrings. The other was short and squatty. The Mexican wore blue satin pants, a black leather vest, but no shirt, and a blue bandana tied in a roll around his head.

I couldn't tell the tone of the conversation because their faces were expressionless, but I didn't like what I saw. If MacClanahan was working intelligence on prison gangs, what was he doing holding a clandestine meeting with four of the baddest looking cons I'd ever seen. If my suspicions were right, I mused, I knew already how the information about the grant money leaked out. MacClanahan had changed sides. Like a police officer who works too long undercover vice or narcotics, he'd lost his identity, misplaced his loyalty, and had slipped into the deviant role as a participant instead of an observer.

Suddenly, a huge black hand flashed in the corner of my right eye. It encased by jaw and neck from behind and jerked me up off the floor. I was spun around in the air and smashed against a stack of pallets. Before I could collect my wits, the hand was under my chin, gripping my jaw like a vice and holding me a foot off the floor. I found myself eye to eye with a giant. His black head was shaved bald. Two diamond earrings hung from his thick lobes, and gold teeth filled the center of his mouth, which was opened in a fiendish smile, like a shark just before it rips apart its helpless prey. His black eyes danced with insane frenzy. He wore skin tight blue nylon warm-up pants and zippered top without sleeves, which only served to display his huge muscles.

He had on rubber thongs for shoes. I was afraid that if he held me this way for long, my neck would stretch and my face would take on a permanent deformity. "Look, friend," I muttered between my teeth. "I think you have the wrong man. I have no money and I'm not after your sister."

His expression didn't change, but he drew me through the air toward him. I could see the muscles in his arms swell and tighten. I was going to be the first human shot-put thrown in a warehouse, I thought. "You're not the real friendly sort, are you?" I muttered.

He jabbed me in the solar plexus with one finger. The wind went out of me entirely and I was sure I was going to heave. Then, he quickly let go of my face and I dropped in a heap on the wooden floor. As I tried to pull myself together. I looked around at the six pair of legs that encircled me, and then looked up into the hard stare of MacClanahan's cold gray eyes. A wry smile broke out on his face and his eyes changed to express the satisfaction of an old mountain lion that had treed the hunter.

"It's all right, Abner," MacClanahan said, looking at the giant figure standing over me. "This is the *egghead* I told you about." Abner broke out in a *basso profundo* laugh, and offered me his hand.

"He's a smart-ass, too, boss. Come on, mon., I won't hurt you. Not now, anyway. Ho... Ho... Ho...," boomed his laughter. Even his speaking tone was loud, deep, and resonant. I thought I could feel the silver fillings in my teeth vibrate when he spoke.

"You're a little lost, aren't you, Worth?" MacClanahan said. "You shouldn't have followed me here. I don't like snoopers." His voice was hard and gravely. "Our contacts are to be by phone only, or a meet in some neutral territory. Now I'll have to re-locate my office."

"Listen, MacClanahan. I just wanted to find out more about the people I will be working with. You just happened to be the easiest to follow from the meeting. There's no need to move. Your location is safe with me."

"You listen, Worth. You checked out okay, but I don't trust anyone. That's how I stay alive. Nothing personal."

I thought he was being a little melodramatic, but didn't want of offend his pride, especially with Abner standing so close. Nevertheless, I didn't want to leave until I was satisfied about what MacClanahan was doing meeting with these hoods.

"I can appreciate your concern, Mac, so you do what you have to do. I'll play it up front with you from now on."

"That's the way I like it, Worth, and I'll treat you with the same respect."

"In that case, Mac, why don't you clarify what's going on here, your meeting with these....a....characters." I gestured toward the four standing behind MacClanahan. I knew I might be over-stepping the limits of our newly formed détente, but I thought he'd respond best to the direct approach.

"Now, Worth, my boy, I thought we reached an understanding, and I was just beginning to like you. You've got nerve, I'll say that, but like I said, I don't like snoopers. I've got my job to do and I'll do it my own way. The minute I have to justify anything to you, it's time I toss in the towel. So, my boy, I suggest you do your thing in Sacramento. I will tell you this, these guys work for me. That's all you need to know. You go separate the good guys from the bad guys, collect your fee, and be on your way."

I could see that the direct approach, or any other approach, would not get me the answers I wanted. I was frustrated and still suspicious, yet I could not help but respect

MacClanahan. He was his own man and expressed the same needs that I had. He did things on his own terms, or not at all. The frustrating aspect of this situation, however, was that to the extent he had control, I didn't. Nevertheless, I understood his position. I was the new kid on the block, and in his mind I was an *egghead*, an academic, and I'd have to prove myself first to earn his respect, then his trust, before any sort of relationship could develop. I decided to leave while my dignity and my body were intact.

Chapter 4

I drove north on 101, back across the Golden Gate Bridge, through Marin County and into Sonoma County, toward Oak Grove. The traffic was light and I drove at a steady 69 mph, just under the radar, to avoid attention from the Highway Patrol. The day was warming nicely, just as the weather girl had predicted, and I rolled down my window all the way and let the wind blow through my hair. It was getting long and beginning to curl in the back. I needed a haircut. The warm air filled the cab and felt clean and good. It looked as though we were in for a hot summer.

I was beginning to doubt the wisdom of accepting this new job offer. *I think you did it again, Matthew,* I said to myself. *I think you got yourself into something above your head. When are you going to learn to think things all the way through before acting? Probably never,* I replied. I seldom take my own advice. *Well, at least it won't be a boring summer. And, $67,000 can pay my bills and extend my independence for quite a while. But what's it all for?*

My old friend Hatfield used to say that life is merely a series of experiences: some are related and some are random, and some you'll like and some you won't. I was curious to see which one this would be.

It seem to me that I had just left San Francisco, when 45 miles later I looked up and saw the Oak Grove exit sign and snapped out of my reverie. I exited right off the freeway and drove north on the old Highway 101, now called Old Redwood Highway, that ran through all the towns in this section of the county before the freeway was built.

To call Oak Grove a town is really stretching the meaning of the word *town*. It's a small village by any standard. It has one main street four blocks long, with Vern's feed store, Angie's grocery and deli, a post office, Mel's barber shop, Fred's welding shop, Fay's video rental store, Bill and Mary's western wear and saddle store, and two bars, along with 1,620 assorted inhabitants, scattered within the radius of a few miles.

Most of the core population were middle aged or older, and most of them lived either in the eight block square residential area on the east side of town or on one of the small ranches that encircled the town. These ranches once were common all over the valley; each with a small sturdy house and several rows of chicken houses trailing off to the rear of the property. Now the chicken houses sat empty, with sunken roofs and hanging doors, ghostly reminders of a different way of life.

Natives of the area would tell you how nice living here used to be before the freeway, and before the developer, one-nail Weston, built the first subdivision in nearby Petaluma in the early 1950s.

Nearly all the flat land around Petaluma, six miles to the south, was subdivided now, right up to the foothills, and the custom builders were attacking those with a vengeance. The town of Petaluma once had a population of 8,000, but now boasted a population of 65,000, and the mayor had the gall to say that the town was growing in all the right ways, an oxymoron at best.

Five miles to the north on what used to be Grover's seed farm, was now Groveland Park, what they called a planned community of about 75,000. How does one plan to grow big and grotesque?

Oak Grove was being surrounded by urban sprawl, but so far it had managed to keep its village atmosphere and country lifestyle. The exception to this was at commute time when hundreds of workers who lived in Santa Rosa, twelve miles to the north, drove down the old highway to the north edge of town and turned at the newly installed light, and headed south along another back road through a portion of the old residential area that lead toward connection roads to the Bay Area. They were all trying to avoid the freeway congestion that always piled up as one approached Petaluma. The reverse scenario occurred during the evening commute.

I lived in a small one-story bungalow-style wood framed house, painted beige with brown trim, with a rusty red composition shingle roof, in Oak Grove's residential area two blocks above the town's main street. The 60 x 150 foot lot was surrounded by a white picket fence that hadn't seen fresh paint in years. A small barn to the rear of the house served as a storage shed, tool crib, and garage. Two huge Golden Delicious apple trees and an old fig tree graced the back yard and two groups of white birch, with three trees each, occupied spaces on the front lawn, equi-distant from the graveled center walk.

A mixture of perennial and annual flowers ringed the lawn areas, and geraniums over-flowed from the window boxes along the front and sides of the house. The property had been willed to me in 2005, in its present condition, by my Aunt Emma, my father's sister. That was one of the main reasons I re-located here, near the Bay area. That, plus the part time teaching opportunities at nearby Sonoma State University, once called Cotati Tech, and several nearby community colleges.

It also allowed me the opportunity to visit my old friend and mentor, Hatfield Gowdy, who lived in Inverness, a village in Marin County, on the west side of Tomales Bay. Fortunately for me, my house was considered as separate property and not community property, so it was never an issue in my divorce.

My aunt had been born and raised here, and had been the local post mistress for 34 years. She knew everyone. As her kin, I had been welcomed as a local by the natives, something that few newcomers experience, I was told. The house came furnished. Two bedrooms, one bathroom with a tub and overhead shower off the hall between the bedrooms, and a half bath with a toilet and sink off the back porch, a small living room, small dining area off the kitchen, and a large screened-in back porch. The front porch was open and ran the width of the house and was covered with the roof overhang. Two old wicker rockers and a wicker two-seater swing sat on the front porch decking.

Inside, the furniture was old, but it was clean, solid and comfortable. My bedroom was relatively large and contained a double bed, with bird's eye maple headboard and matching dresser, chest of drawers, and two matching nightstands.

The second bedroom contained a similar set made of light oak. The rest of the furniture was a mixture of oak and mahogany. The old Morris chair in the living room was my favorite. The wooden arms swung up sideways on hinges, revealing storage compartments that were each sufficiently large enough to hold a quart of *Jose Cuervo* undetected, if one would want to put them there. The small kitchen featured an old, but clean, Wedgewood gas stove and a Crosley refrigerator. A 4 x 4 chrome table with a Formica top fit snuggly in the corner near the rear window. A large window over the sink looked out onto the side yard.

It was a comfortable house, and I liked living here.

Chapter 5

As I approached the house, I saw a late model Subaru SUV parked in the driveway. I didn't recognize the car and I wasn't expecting any visitors, but then I never expect visitors. I parked my pickup behind the Subaru, got out, grabbed the bag containing my dirty socks and shorts, and started cautiously toward the front door.

The door opened and there she was, Libby, my ex-wife.

"Libby! What a surprise!" I shuddered. "To what do I owe the pleasure?" I said sarcastically. "What are you doing here?"

"Hi Zee. I missed you." She had always been intrigued by my middle name, Zeno, and called me Zee, her pet name for me.

"Libby. What do you want? How did you get in?" I walked onto the porch, but kept my distance. She looked tired and thinner than I remembered her, and there was gauntness about her face. Her right hand was placed high on one of the poles that ran from the porch to the roof support and her hips were slung to the left, trying to accentuate the roundness of her cheeks, but there was a bagginess in her pants that I hadn't seen before. She was wearing powder blue jeans and a tight-fitting black cotton sweater. She looked appealing, even in her present physical condition, and for just a short moment I felt a slight twinge in my groin. However, I quickly returned to reality and knew that her appearance meant trouble.

"You always did know how to work a guy, Libby."

"What.......?" Her voice had an overlay of false innocence.

"I asked why you are here. What do you want, Libby?"

"One question at a time, Zee. How about a hug for old time sake?" She moved to me and we hugged briefly before I could react otherwise. "It's good to see you, Zee. I was in the neighborhood so thought I would stop by to see you. You weren't here, but I remembered that you always kept the door key on the top sill, so I let myself in. And here I am."

"I can see that Libby. Just happened to be in the neighborhood. Sure, and I'm going to win the lottery tonight. You want something, Libby, you always do. "

"Don't be so suspicious, Zee. Aren't you going to ask me inside for some coffee, or a beer, or something?"

"Sure, Libby, why don't you come on in for a cup of coffee, a beer, or something, then tell me what you want." I tried not to sound condescending or angry, yet I wanted to tell her to get the hell out of my life, and stay out.

I had thought things were going so great with us after we married. We even talked once about starting a family. Then one day, about two years into our marriage, she said she had to find herself, and she left. I didn't hear from her for almost six months, and when I did she was living in Reno with some cop I once knew, and she needed money. Later, I found out that shortly after we were married and I had encouraged her to get to know some of my friends, she took me literally, in the Biblical sense, if you know what I mean, and got to *know* several.

The hurt was too much to deal with at first, and I started drinking heavily. After about six months of numbness, I stopped feeling sorry for myself, cleaned up, and returned to part-time work. Also, I began to experience a wonderful sense of freedom and independence in being single. I also stopped blaming her, but I still did not want to have her back in my life again.

We went into the kitchen, "Have a seat, Libby," I said, trying to sound somewhat sociable, and pointed to one of the chairs on the far side of the chrome and Formica table. I took two Heineken's from the refrigerator, popped the lids, and handed her one, as I took a seat in the chair opposite her. I noticed that her hair was now blonde, but I didn't mention it.

"Well, Zee, it's been awhile," she said, trying to sound casual.

"You look good, Libby. How've you been?" In this lighting and up close she actually looked tired and dissipated, as if she had been on a long binge.

"To be honest with you, Zee, not too good." Her tone took on a mood of depression and became softer. "I've been living out of my car the past three months, staying in various county or state parks at night. Doing odd jobs here and there for food money. My luck went south, and I am about as down and out as anyone could ever be.

I was surprised at her frankness. "So that's it, huh, Libby. That's why you showed up here, thinking I'd give you some sort of handout for old time sake." I tried to sound unemotional and hold back the bitterness, but some of it leaked through.

"I'm sorry, Zee. I have no place else to go. No one else to turn to. I don't want a handout. I just need a place to rest up for a few days. I won't be a problem, I promise. Hey, I'll even cook for you, clean the house, and wash your clothes, just like it used to be." She forced a perky smile.

"Hold it, Libby." I stood up slowly and put up my right hand as a stop sign gesture. "It's never going to be *like it used to be*."

"I know, Zee. I don't blame you. You have every right to throw me out, but please, Zee, just let me stay for a few days. I'll take the spare bedroom, and you won't even know I'm here." She was actually pleading. Something she had never done with me before, or was it just a fake.

While she was talking and looking at me with those big deep green eyes, I thought *why not help her out for a few days. You're not going to be here anyway and she could keep an eye on the place for you. Might be doing you a favor, and what harm can come from that. She could even stay for a month or so, until she could get herself back into some form of healthy condition.*

"I'll tell you what, Libby, it just so happens that I am going to be staying in Sacramento for a month or two on a job, maybe for the summer. I have taken an apartment there and will only be home on an occasional weekend. I could use someone to look after the house. You can stay for a month or so on three conditions: One, that you don't have any stay-over company; two, that you don't drink hard liquor while you're here; and three, that you don't come on to me while I'm here. You can keep the place clean and cook for me when I do come home, but you're just a guest, a short-term guest."

"Oh, and Libby, don't change the curtains or rearrange the furniture."

"Oh Zee, you're too kind. I won't be a problem and I'll do what you ask." She was trying to sound assured, but she looked me intently looking for some reaction, some cues to how I really felt about her return. I gave her none.

What she said sounded corny and contrived, but her spirits seemed to pick up and she did look grateful. Looking back on this scene later, I came to understand that when you give a person conditions, or even suggestions, they should never be stated in the negative, always in the positive. Never say *don't do*, only what they should do. *But what did I know?*

Chapter 6

I spent the afternoon mowing the front lawn and picking up around the yard, while Libby actually Hoovered the floors and did the dishes I had left in the sink. Late in the afternoon, I brought home two Italian hero sandwiches and a quart of potato salad from Angie's Deli. The salad was made from a secret recipe given to Angie by Gaetano Perinonni, when he retired from his own deli in Petaluma. The secret was in the home-made mayonnaise, and the salad was like none other could ever be.

We ate in near silence, washing down the food with a smooth *Forchini* Zinfandel from their Dry Creek appellation, while we watched an old *noir*, *Caught*, a film from my collection. It starred Robert Ryan and Ida Lupino. The pursuit scenes through the snow and the transformation of Ryan from a rogue cop to an almost caring person were the highlights.

When it comes to movies and music, I am a throwback to the 1930's and 40's, an atavist, if you will. I knew that Libby was bored, but she didn't let on, and she pretended to enjoy the movie. Neither of us could finish our hero sandwiches or the salad, so I wrapped them back up and put them in the refrigerator. Libby finished the wine.

I let Libby get ready for bed first, using the bathroom, while I packed for my stay in Sacramento. I planned to leave first thing in the morning. I packed two suitcases and a garment bag with everything I thought I'd need for two months, including my laptop and my small HP laser printer.

My Colt .380 Mustang was still in my boot. It is so small and unobtrusive that I had forgotten about it. I threw it in the second suitcase. It was one of two handguns I was licensed by the sheriff to carry concealed. The second one was a new Mateba Model 6 Unica made in Italy. I had recently purchased it from a gun dealer in Florida and transferred title through a local gun dealer friend of mine. It's a .357 cal., and is the only automatic revolver manufactured in the world today. It came with interchangeable four and six inch barrels.

I bought it with both the four inch and six inch barrels, but routinely carried it with the four inch barrel. It was fashioned after the old English Webley-Fosbery eight-shot .38 cal. automatic revolver design patented in 1897, by Col. Fosbery of the East Indies Regiment, and made by the British firm of Webley & Scott from 1901 to 1914. Only 300 of them were manufactured because they jammed in combat, but they were highly valued in marksman exhibitions because of their accuracy.

I became intrigued with the Webley-Fosbery when I saw it used by Mary Astor to kill Archer, Sam Spade's detective partner, in the movie, *The Maltese Falcon*, and was absolutely sold on the style when I saw Sean Connery use it so deftly in the 1973 movie, *Zardoz*. I was also certain that it was the side arm worn by Stewart Granger in the 1950 film, *King Solomon's Mines* and by Jack Baker in *Zulu*. The gun used in these later movies might actually have been just a Webley, but the romantic in me added the Fosbery features.

Since the Webley-Fosbery hadn't been made since 1914, I settled for the Italian Mateba, which actually is a superb handgun, far superior to the Webley. It functions like a regular double action revolver with the first trigger pull. However, upon firing, the upper part of the frame recoils, automatically cocking the hammer and rotating the cylinder. Thereafter it fires just like an automatic.

The gun cost me $1,600, plus the registration and local dealer fees. I placed the gun in the suitcase, with its shoulder holster, and a box of .357 ammunition. I wasn't a gun nut, but I did enjoy target shooting, and occasionally thought it necessary to carry concealed during particularly sensitive private investigations. *Ah, men and their toys,* I mused.

Libby yelled a muffled "Goodnight, Zee. I'm through in the bathroom."

"Thanks, Libby. Goodnight."

Sometime during the night, about 2:00 a.m. I think, I felt the covers move and Libby slid her body under the covers and alongside mine. She was naked. For just a moment, she felt good; close and warm. She smelled good too, with just the right mixture of perfume and body scent. I was tempted for just that moment, but then reality struck again. I pulled the covers back off of Libby and said, "Libby, remember the condition. You don't hit on me. It's not going to happen. Now go back to you own bed."

"OK, Zee. I know. I just thought… you know…."

"Yes, I know….*for old time sake*. Well, the old times are gone, Libby, so let them go. You have to let them go," She sighed and left the room. I'm sure that we both stayed hot for a long time.

Chapter 7

Before leaving for Sacramento Saturday morning, I went to see Perry Schaller, a retired high school woodshop teacher who lived next door. No one answered the door so I walked around to the back yard and found him in his barn that he had converted into a woodshop. It housed all the latest woodworking tools.

Perry was a short and slightly built man with muscled arms and slightly bowed legs. His graying hair was always neatly combed and parted down the middle and back in a wave on each side. Although Perry had retired as a woodshop teacher, he spent most of his waking hours out in his workshop either building or repairing furniture for others. Also, he was one of the last chair caners living in the area.

"Hey Perry," I called out in advance of walking up on him. He jumped, as if slightly startled, and turned toward me with that broad warm smile that he always had at the ready. "What are you working on?"

"Caning, Matt, I am going to cane this old wooden captain's chair. Come, let me show you. "

I attended his side, with the best attentive look I could muster, as I always did when Perry wanted to display his talents, which he often did.

"See Matt," Perry said, holding up a wheel of cane. "This is called a "hank" or 1,000 feet of cane. I use about 250-300 feet to cane a chair seat with about 80 holes. I'm getting ready to prepare the cane by cutting individual lengths and rolling each individual strand & clipping them with clothespins, being sure not to kink or twist the cane. This helps get a feel for the cane, its eyes, its growth direction and it also makes the cane easier to soak. Next, I'll soak the cane in warm water with a couple of capfuls of Glycerin for seventeen minutes before it's ready to use. Then I'll trim each strand on an angle to make it easier to thread in the holes. When I get to these corners here, I'll use the needle-nose pliers to pull the strands through the tight places. I'm almost ready to start, Matt. I can't multi-task, so once I begin, I won't be able to continue our conversation."

"O.K., Perry. Thanks for the lesson. I'll make my stay short." Once Perry got started explaining a project, he wouldn't stop until the task was complete. I quickly explained my job in Sacramento and told him I would be gone for a month or two and explained to him about Libby's presence. I gave him my cell phone number and asked him to phone me if Libby had any men show up. I also asked him to mind the garden and chase away any strangers, both of which he relished doing.

"Sure, Matt, "I'd be happy to. I know you've talked about Libby as your ex, but I have not had the pleasure of meeting her. Actually, I am surprised that you are taking her in, given the way in which you described your life together." Perry always was direct. "Tell her I'm here, Matt, and that I'll come over later and introduce myself. We can keep each other company while you're away."

"Thanks, Perry, but don't get any ideas about Libby. She's only here for as long as I am away, by which time she will be back on her feet and be off on her own." I left Perry to his caning ritual.

I had intended to phone the local paper to stop my subscription, but I thought that having it to read might help Libby pass the time. As I recalled, she was easily bored. I left the phone service on, of course, and took comfort in the fact that I did not have a long distance carrier as a part of the phone service. I used my cell phone for any long distance calls, and still had several hundred roll-over minutes left on my AT & T wireless account.

I said goodbye to Libby. "Take care, Libby. My neighbor, Perry will come over one of these days to introduce himself. He's a nice guy and he watches out for my place when I am away. Call him if you need anything. I'll be in touch."

I felt that she wanted a hug or some sort of real touching before I left, but I smiled, turned and walked to my pickup truck. I had to maintain the distance between us.

Chapter 8

I drove out of the driveway and headed south on Adobe Road, then east on Stage Gulch Road, past the Sonoma and Napa cutoffs, and intercepted Highway 80 going east toward Sacramento.

I made it to Sacramento in just under two hours, and after ten minutes of fighting with one-way streets and new *cul-de-sacs*, I located my new apartment complex. It consisted of twenty Spanish style apartment units in a secluded area overlooking the Sacramento River. Imitation adobe walls, machine hewn timbers, and synthetic tile roofs were neatly arranged to provide the utmost privacy. A well-manicured lawn, with twelve olive trees, a tennis court, and a small fenced-in pool occupied the grounds.

I found my apartment in the middle of the complex, ground floor. The synthetic Spanish motif was carried out inside: white stucco walls, heavy wooden furniture, and brightly colored tapestries and wall prints as decorations. I like the Spanish style, but this was a bit over-done and lacked any real substance.

There was one large bedroom with a separate bath and vanity area. The shower was large enough for group bathing, or whatever.

I was already missing the homey atmosphere of my own house, even with Libby in it. There was something sterile, something plastic about this one, and I was glad it was only a part of the job; only temporary. I unpacked and walked around the living room and kitchen, then walked out the rear sliding door onto a walled-in patio area, with a 6 by 8 foot concrete slab. Looking over the wall, I could see the Sacramento River. Two boys were fishing from a skiff near the bridge.

There was a tennis court and pool in the center of the complex, but they were empty. However, two blonds and a redhead in skimpy suits lay prone, face down on mats on the pool deck sunning themselves. A well-tanned and well-built woman in her late twenties was sitting in a lawn chair reading a paperback. She looked up and smiled. I smiled back. After a few minutes, she put her book down, smiled again, and rolled off the chair onto the cement decking, laying on her stomach, exposing her back side. She had long tear-drop cheeks with a little sag in them. I preferred them round, full, and firm.

As I walked back into my apartment, my stomach gurgled. It was nearly 5:00 p.m. and I realized that I hadn't eaten anything since that leftover hero sandwich I ate early this morning. I returned to my apartment and looked around the kitchen and saw there was no food. I don't know what I was expecting.

I found a Raley's supermarket within a few blocks and loaded up a large cart, and made my way through the line to the checkout counter. The checker, a trim blond in her late 30's, was one of those commentator types that requires conversation with every customer, whenever she wasn't talking with one of her co-checkers

"Your turn to do the shopping huh?" she asked.

"Yes," I replied. I didn't feel like conversation.

"Wow, you must be having a barbecue or party with all this steak, beer, chips, and booze."

"Not really, I eat like this all the time." It is at times like this that I wished I'd put a large tube of Preparation-H or a pack of giant sized condoms in the grocery basket.

"This cheap stuff any good?" she asked, holding up one of the two bottles of *Jose Cuervo* I'd put in the cart.

"I don't care what it costs. If it's good, I want it. Don't you?"

"Yeh, I know what you mean," she replied, as if she understood, but her eyes took on a glassy look. At least she stopped her commentary.

I paid with my debit card, wheeled the cart out to my truck, unloaded the bags of groceries into the back, and drove back to the apartment. I tried to carry three bags at once, but the third bag ripped open, dumping frozen vegetables, chips, and meat packages all over the truck bed. Damn, they don't even make real bags anymore. I struggled with the remaining two bags to my apartment and noticed that the door was slightly ajar. I pushed it open and walked in, still holding the two bags of groceries.

No one was in the apartment, but the sliding door to the patio was open. I put the bags on the counter and walked out onto the patio. The wrought iron gate separating my patio from the pool deck area was standing open. The three sunbathing girls were now splashing in the pool. Tear-drop cheeks was gone.

I returned to my truck, brought in the rest of the groceries and put them away. I dumped some ice cubes in a four-ounce glass and filled it with tequila, and sang, *Jose Cuervo, you are a friend of mine.*

I figured out how to operate the built-in electric barbecue, trimmed a small porterhouse steak, sliced a red onion and some mushrooms, and was about to prepare a salad when the doorbell rang. I set the steak aside, took a gulp of tequila, walked over and opened the door. It was the girl from the pool, Tear-Drop cheeks, wearing her revealing bathing suit. She was tall, about 5' 7", firm and beautifully proportioned all over. The afternoon sun coming through the patio door danced around the room and created an intense catch-light in her coal-black eyes.

"Hi neighbor, I'm Carla Renati." She walked past me into the living room. "I live in No. 4. I saw you move in today. What's your name?"

"I'm Matthew Worth, but you can call me Matt. Everyone does." I followed her cheeks with my eyes as she walked around, staring for a moment into my bedroom, then she walked into the living area and turned toward me. She had a beautiful doll-like round face, deep set black eyes, and an impish smile on her face.

"Nice place you have. Just like mine. Since you're new here I just thought I'd stop by and say hello. If there's anything you need to know about the place, just give a holler. See you later."

She was gone, cheeks bouncing out the door. Damn, just when I was ready to accept the tear-drop look. I wondered why she really had come. From my experience, sweet young things just don't drop by to welcome their neighbors. I walked into the bedroom and looked around. My briefcase had been opened and the contents were scattered about the bed. The dresser drawers had been pulled out and dumped upside down on the carpet.

I replaced the drawers, picked up my clothes and papers, and examined the contents of my briefcase. There was nothing of value there and nothing seemed to be missing. My Colt .380 and Mateba .357 were tucked safely in my usual hiding place, under a large frying pan I had placed in the dishwasher.

Strange, the break-in so obvious, and Carla's long stare into my bedroom, as if she was telling me something. I slipped the .380 into the front of my belt, let my shirt hang out to cover it, and went to find Carla Renati.

I rang the bell at No. 4. A sharp and nervous terrier responded immediately with a high pitched yipping. The door opened to the security chain and a small, frumpy, middle aged woman with her hair up in a net appeared. "Yes, what do you want?" she demanded, in a whining voice.

"Who is it Sarah?" a male voice called from within the apartment.

"I'm looking for Carla Renati," I said. "I was told she lived in No. 4."

"This is the Swanson apartment. No Carla lives here." She slammed the door. The dog continued yipping.

I returned to my apartment, finished my tequila and poured another. *No trouble for me, huh? No danger? Just open relationships and cursory investigations, huh? Matt, you did it. Just think, you could be lazing in the back yard hammock or sailing across Tomales Bay in your sloop. But no, you had to be smart and let yourself get sucked into some bureaucratic Keystone Kop adventure. Matt, when are you ever going to learn?* Probably never, I mused.

I thought that some good music would settle me down for the evening and would provide some mood music for my dinner. I found a CD player that held six CDs and loaded it with some of my favorites that I had brought with me: *Moonlight Blues,* with trumpeter Cecil Welch; the hot sax of Joel Edward; the jazz renditions of classic favorites by Diana Krall; Steve Tyrell; and Madeleine Peyroux, and ended with my favorite singer, Julia Rich, a *chanteuse extraordinaire.*

I finished preparing my food, and dined slowly, washing the food down with a bottle of *Mill Creek* Zinfandel. As I finished, Julia Rich was singing one of the last songs on the CD, *I Know Why, and So Do You.* The song was made unusually beautiful by the Gary Weaver arrangement, featuring the sweet trombone sounds of Larry O'Brien. As I recall, it was written by Mack Gordon and Harry Warren for the 1941 movie. *Sun Valley Serenade.* The song was made more meaningful when, as Julia Rich sang the last verse, O'Brien played the last lines of *At Last*, another Gordon/Warren song written for *Orchestra Wives.* What a great touch. Beautiful!

I finished the last of the wine, felt contented, and went to bed.

Chapter 9

I awoke early Sunday morning at the sound of the morning paper thumping against my door. I checked and found a copy of the *Sacramento Bee*. What service. Either Jessup had started a subscription for me or hadn't stopped the original subscription that James had.

I made a pot of coffee, prepared a blender of rum fizzes, and returned to bed to read the paper. The rum was from a ten-case supply that a friend who worked in U. S. Customs had arranged to have shipped to me directly from the Brugal Rum Factory in the Dominican Republic. One hundred and fifty proof, with the best rum taste and texture I'd ever experienced. It was best served straight over ice, but occasionally I indulged myself with a morning fizz, and had brought two liter bottles with me.

As I opened the business section of the paper, someone knocked on the patio door, then slid it open and entered my apartment. Apparently, I had neglected to lock the door last night. I looked up as footsteps padded toward the bedroom door. It was Tear-Drop cheeks.

"Carla, What the Hell...?"

"Good morning, Matt. I thought you'd be up early so I stopped by to see it you'd like to go jogging with me this morning." She was wearing shorts, a sweat shirt, and jogging shoes.

"Where in the hell did you go the other night?" I asked. My tone was pleasant, but curious. "I went to No. 4 and they never heard of you."

"Oh," she interrupted. "I live in No. 4 over there, the apartment complex next door. It's identical to this one. Same developers, you know, and we share the pool and tennis court."

She left the bedroom and returned with a glass from the kitchen, and poured herself a fizz from the blender on the nightstand. She climbed onto the bed and squatted facing me next to my hip, letting her right leg lay across my stomach.

She sipped her fizz. "Come on, Matt, jog with me. You'll feel better afterwards."

"Sorry, honey," I replied, "about the best I can do is to jog my memory in the morning on the way to the bathroom." While I was talking, I lay my hand on her upper leg. Her flesh was soft and warm. She looked me up and down.

"Do you always sleep in the nude?" She asked quietly.

"Yeh, I can't stand pajamas. They're too restricting. I might get all twisted up during the night and cut off the circulation."

"That would be just horrible," she responded, with a delightful twinkle in her eye.

I didn't mind her being the aggressor. In fact, I like assertive women because they can express themselves honestly without including a critical putdown of others, and usually they can take honesty back without the display of righteous indignation. And it wasn't that I objected to a romp in the sack in the morning either. It's one of the best times. It was just that I didn't know Carla yet, and with rare exception, I needed to know a woman first and to feel an emotional intimacy with her, before sex became completely enjoyable. I also am very cautious when anyone tries to be too friendly toward me for no reason, and even more so, considering my current situation. And, when I looked deep within, I felt pangs of potential betrayal to Libby. *How foolish was that?*

I looked at Carla. She was kneeling, now, on the bed with her back straight, but bent at the waist toward me. The vee of her sweatshirt sagged down revealing the fullness of her beautifully proportioned breasts, creamy white with big pinkish-brown nipples. She moved toward me a little and her breasts moved ever so slightly and began to harden.

"Come on, Carla, I'd better jog with you while I still have the energy."

We jogged south along the Sacramento River on a path through one of those man-made fitness trails, ignoring the exercise contraptions. Carla radiated an air of beauty and excitement, like a captured wild horse finally set free. Her body was firm; I could tell because the tear-drop cheeks snapped back and forth, rather than undulating in circles as she jogged. Those were not just ordinary snaps, I decided. Those were power snaps, if I'd ever seen any.

I hated jogging; it's so boring. Nevertheless, I managed to keep stride with her for about two miles. Finally, I ran out of gas. I had to rest, so I sat on an old stump and threw rocks into the river, while she ran on. The river looked clean and inviting, and the water skiers and fishermen seemed to be sharing it with mutual respect.

After about twenty minutes, I heard a runner coming and turned to see her sprinting toward me. He breasts bounced slightly under her sweatshirt, held in check by a sports bra that she had slipped on before we left the apartment. A morning breeze blew her coal-black hair in all directions. The catch-light in her eyes was again dazzling.

"Come on, Matt. Ill race you back to the apartment," she yelled, as she ran up to me, pulled me backwards off the stump, laughed, and ran on.

"Why you little devil. I'll show you a thing or two about running." But try as I might, I couldn't catch her.

When I finally reached my apartment, Carla was sprawled in the middle of the living room rug, laughing between taking deep breaths of air.

"Laugh at me, will you," and I fell to the floor with my hands around her waist and began tickling her. Her laughter came freely, and it was rich and full. Then, suddenly, she made a few moves and I found myself flat on my back with her straddling my chest.

"Now it's my turn, you poor sport. Can't stand the thought of losing to a woman, huh?", and then and she found all my tickle spots.

We rolled around the rug, tickling and laughing for several minutes, then looked at each other like two adolescents coming together in those awkward moments of first intimacy. Finally, we both stopped, exhausted, and rolled over on our backs to catch our breath.

"How about a shower?" she said, offering me her best carnal smile.

I was caught short momentarily, not knowing what to answer or how I should answer. Opportunities like this don't come along often in one's life. Then, I had a reality check. *Watch yourself, Matthew. Things are never as they seem. This is probably to set you up for something. You better divert the course of human nature until you know what the real nature of it is.*

I got up off the floor and straightened out my sweats. "Sorry, Carla. Maybe at a later time when we know each other better. I don't do well under so sudden an on-rush of expectation." I had to make up some excuse.

She looked surprised, at first, then displayed a pout, then smiled and said, "Sure Matt. I understand. Too assertive for you, huh? You want to be the one to initiate the action?"

She used up-talk on her last comment so that it sounded like a question instead of a statement of fact. Nevertheless, my first reaction was to respond with *why is it that you women always think men want to be in charge? I'm no control freak, but....I just....Cool it, Matthew. Let it rest as it lies.*

I responded with, "Let's just say that I'm old fashioned and it's too soon in a relationship, if there is going to be a relationship. So let's cool off for now and see how it plays out, shall we?" I tried to throw it back on her in the form of a question at the end, and I used my *I need understanding* tone.

She responded with a smile somewhere between cute and sheepish. "You got it, Matt. You're right, damn it." I'll be back shortly, if that's O.K?"

"Sure, Carla. Sounds good to me. I'll shower and see you in about fifteen."

She vanished out the patio door. I showered, shaved, and dressed in clean gray cut-offs and my favorite dark blue tee-shirt from Carmel that had the name *Hogs Breath Inn* on the back. The thought crossed my mind at the time I was showering that *you know, there really is room in this shower for two.*

Chapter 10

Carla popped in through the patio door, looking fresh, and wearing a warm but seemingly harmless smile. I made a fresh batch of rum fizzes, while Carla prepared an omelet with onions, peppers, mushrooms, sliced sausage, and lots of cheddar cheese, and prepared what I call butter-fried hash brown potatoes in another fry pan.   Might as well get our calories and trans fat for the day out of the way.

We sat at one of the small tables that was on the patio and ate and drank and talked. She talked about what she did, but not about who she was. Whenever my probing got too close to her, she laughed or offered some clever comment, and quickly led me away to things outside of herself.

She had worked for eight months as a speech writer and media relations person for Governor Osborne during his campaign last year. He was then the mayor of Freeport, a large city south of Los Angeles, and was running on a strong law-and-order ticket. She had been very useful, he told her, in softening the tone of his campaign to appeal to a wider audience without weakening the conservative support of his own party. He liked her work, and brought her to Sacramento as his public information person and appointment secretary when he assumed office last January.

"You're an unusual girl, Carla. You come into my life from nowhere, move in close and personal, initially, and now you seem content to sit here the rest of the day discussing politics. Who are you? What do we have going on here? And, how did you know I was using this apartment?" I thought the direct approach would be best to try and get a show of feelings.

"I'm just your common run-of-the-mill single girl, Matt. Nothing special. But to tell you the truth, I knew that our office leased this apartment and that someone was coming in yesterday. Since I live so close, I was curious, so thought I'd check out whoever it would be. When I saw it was you, I liked what I saw. I'm my own person, a free person, and when I see something I want, I go after it. You look like something I want."

Can't get any more direct than that, I thought, but it bothered me that she knew about the apartment and my coming, especially since Jessup assured me that only those within the select circle knew what I was about. I wondered what else Carla knew. *OK, now Matthew, how do you respond to this?*

"Well thanks, Carla. It's nice to be wanted, I think. What else do you know about me and what I'm doing here?"

"That's all, Matt. All I know is that our office maintains the lease on this apartment, and several others around the city, for use by special consultants or project managers working on a temporary contract basis. I really never know who uses the apartments or what they are doing. What are you going to be doing, Matt?"

She threw the ball back to me. "I'll be working with the Board of Corrections as a consultant on the new community corrections grant. At this point, that's all I know myself. I'll have to see what the job entails as I entail it." I used my moderate sarcastic tone, with a casual overlay. No sense pushing this. If she knows, she will just give me some cover story. If she doesn't know, I don't need to tell her. We left it at that.

Chapter 11

I decided to check in with my old friend, confident, and mentor, Hatfield Gowdy, and fill him in on my situation. He is always available when I need information, or just advice. He worked with my dad in the mines in Gabbs and Ely, Nevada, and had always been like a second father to me. He left the mines shortly after my dad died, and has mentored me ever since in life's adventure.

Hat now lives in a small cottage in Inverness, up in back of the village, on what is called the Mesa, near the elementary school, and high above the tennis courts. Although he is about seventy years of age, he is lean, hard, and agile, with thick graying hair and a pencil thin mustache, *the Boston Blackie kind.* He looks to be the outdoor type, but now spends most of his time in front of a computer; a whiz he is.

I called and got his answering machine. "Hi Hat, this is Matt. I just wanted to check in and…….."

He picked up his receiver, "Matthew, my boy, I thought it might be you."

"What were you doing, Hat, screening your calls?"

"You're right, Matthew. I was right in the middle of a letter to the editor and didn't want to be interrupted by just anyone."

"What is it this time, Hat?"

"What do you mean?"

"If you're writing to an editor, I know you are complaining about something amiss in society that you plan to correct," I said, with a sarcastic tone that I knew he would appreciate.

"Ah Matthew, my boy, such is my lot in life, to discover the social ills that others ignore, and to edify those willing to listen."

"O.K., Hat, but exactly what ills are you addressing this time?"

"Well Matthew, people, especially young people, have become slovenly in their speech patterns, and right now I'm focusing on the use of the preposition *at*. Too many people use it at the end of a sentence: *Where's he at?- Where're you at? - I don't know where I'm at.* I hear sportscasters say it all the time, and other radio announcers too. They don't seem to know that they are really saying: *Where is he at ? Where are you at? I don't know where I am at.*" Drop the *at*. They sound like hillbillies, fresh off the truck. They should know too never end a sentence in a preposition, especially *at*."

"I see, Hat. You have taken on quite a task, correcting people's speech jargon. I wish you all the best in your endeavor." I had a slight sarcastic and mocking tone in my voice, knowing full well that Hat would continue jabbing at the use of words by those un-anointed by his grace.

"Well, Matthew, someone has to do it. And you know that no one does it better than I. Now, Matthew, what brings you to my door, as it were?"

I filled Hat in on the details of my latest job assignment and on Libby's reappearance in my life. He listened without interruption, although I heard him typing on the computer while he half-listened.

"I always liked Libby, Matthew. She was vibrant and alive, and she made you alive too. However, I remember what she did to you, although she wasn't fully to blame. You were no angel at that time, as I remember. In fact, you might have led the way for her to follow. I also know that you often thought with the head in your pants and not the one on your shoulders, so heed my advice and don't throw her out, but move slowly with any reconciliation efforts."

"I'm with you on that score, Hat. I have no plans to reconcile, and I expect her to move on once she gets re-fueled at my house. She was never one to stay settled for long. I'll keep you posted, Hat. And Hat, if I send you an e-mail with several names on it, will you check them out for me?"

"Sure, Matthew, any time."

"Say Hat, is that neighbor lady, Mrs. Berwick, still coming over to keep you warm at night?"

"No, she's mad at me and hasn't been over in two weeks."

"What did you do, Hat, complain about her cooking?"

"No Matthew, I awoke from my nap late one afternoon and found her rearranging the furniture and sorting out the folders on my desk. I gave her my usual oxen bellow and chased her out of the house, if it's any of your business."

"My, my Hat, you sure know how to handle women." But I knew exactly how he felt. I would have done the same thing.

"You know that I don't like anyone trying to take over my life, and changing the furniture is the first step. Next thing you know she'll be wanting to straighten out my files and clean off the top of my dresser." He was trying to sound sarcastic, but I knew that he really meant it. He was afraid of losing control, and his concern seemed to increase with age.

"I know what you mean, Hat, but an explanation might have worked better than a loud bellow."

"Matthew, enough !"

"Sorry Hat. I didn't mean to meddle."

"When are you going to come see me? We'll take your sailboat out and make a day of it."

"As soon as this situation in Sacramento gets settled. Maybe in a week or so. I can use a day of doing nothing. I'll keep in touch, Hat."

Chapter 12

God knows how I hate Mondays. And the idea of working five eight hour days didn't thrill me either. Nevertheless, I got up, started the coffee and completed my shave, shower, and toilet ritual. I ate a quick breakfast: apple juice, a bagel cheeseburger, and three cups of black coffee. I dressed in my blue-gray *Levi* three-piece suit, old, but clean, and drove to my new job at the Board of Corrections (BOC) building.

I arrived at 7:45 a.m. The lights were on inside and the door was unlocked. The building outside was gray cement construction that now looked old and weathered. The important politicians had taken the new office buildings and relegated these old ones to various bureaucratic boards and commissions. The Board of Corrections was on the ground floor, south wing. I entered and heard the sound of a dicta-phone being played back in one of the offices. I thought that those contraptions were long gone. I called out, "Anyone home?"

The machine clicked off, a chair squeaked and the sound of high heels came toward me from inside the front office. "Dr. Worth, I presume."

"Yes, I'm Matthew Worth." I walked toward her and held out my hand.

"I'm Mary Reed-Wilder, Dr. Worth. Welcome aboard."

She was about 45 years old, with neatly styled gray-tinted black hair, wearing a tailored blue and white checkered pants suit, silver-framed half-rim glasses that drew attention to the dark blue eye shadow, and large silver-hoop earrings. She did not wear any rings; a feature of a woman that I notice now on a regular basis, ever since Libby had explained its importance in sizing up women. She was a large-framed woman, about 150 pounds, but she carried it well.

"A pleasure to meet you Ms. Wilder. I look forward to working with you." She took my hand, and her face broke into a smile, but her hazel eyes were stone cold. "It's Reed-Wilder, not Wilder. I can appreciate your enthusiasm for the new job, Dr. Worth, and I know why you're here. But, you need to understand one thing. You will be working *for* me, not *with* me."

She turned and walked down to the end of the counter which separated the small lobby from the office area, pushed open the wooden swinging door, and gestured down the hall.

"Come in, Dr. Worth   Let me show you to your office." She was still smiling with her mouth, but her eyes were still stone cold.

She opened the door and entered the fourth door down the hall, walked to the window, and pulled open the drapes, letting in the morning sun. The office looked directly out onto the street. "Here you are, Dr. Worth, your work is ready and waiting." She gestured toward three stacks of folders neatly arranged in the center of the blotter covering a gray metal desk. "As you know, three weeks from this Friday is the closing date to receive grant applications. So far, we've received twelve. I've sorted them for your review, according to geographic areas within the state. We are required to make the grant awards by August 15, and I need four days to review your final recommendations. That gives you six weeks to complete your investigations."

"I wasn't aware that the time constraints were that tight."

"We are operating under federal guidelines, Dr. Worth, as you know. I am responsible to distribute the funds and implement a monitoring program by September 1st. We have sufficient support staff in a steno pool upstairs to handle any clerical needs you might have, and a state car has been requisitioned for you. The keys and a state credit card are in the top drawer of your desk, and the car is parked in the garage across the street, stall No. 31. You can also use your own vehicle, if you choose to do so. Please let me know if I can be of any assistance. And, now, Dr. Worth, if you will excuse me, I have an organization to run."

She turned and was gone before I could respond. Not that there was anything to which I could respond. She had made it clear that she was in charge and that I was her lackey, like all the other employees here. This wasn't starting off like I had expected. Jessup was to meet me here and make the introductions. *Just what is my role really going to be?*

I picked up the phone and called Jessup's office number. He hadn't arrived at work yet, his secretary said, but she'd have him return my call as soon as he came in.

Well, I might as well get to work. I took off my coat and loosened my tie, sat down, and read the federal guidelines on qualifying the applicants that Ms. Reed-Wilder had so thoughtfully left on my desk. The guidelines were detailed in ten pages of complex legalese. Fortunately, someone had attached a two paragraph summary which clearly explained the important features and dates, and which took only ten minutes to read and understand.

The phone buzzed at my desk. I picked it up, "Yes?"

"This is Jill McCloud at the reception desk. You have a call on line two."

"Why thank you, Jill." She sounded delightful over the phone. I'll have to go out and meet her soon. I pushed the flashing button on the phone panel, "Matthew Worth here."

"What do you mean by calling me at my office?" It was Jessup, obviously irritated. "Don't you understand, we're not supposed to know each other? We can't talk like this, it's..."

"Listen, Jessup," I interrupted his blubbering. "I told you once that I don't like surprises."

"What do you mean?"

"Mary Reed-Wilder, that's what I mean. Ms. Efficiency. How much does she know?"

"She knows nothing, only that you're a special consultant on loan from the Federal Office of Criminal Justice Planning. That you'll be investigating the applicants to determine their qualifications, and then recommend who should receive the grant awards."

"What else does she know?"

"That's all, I think." His voice hesitated.

"What do you mean, 'you think'? Damn it Jessup, either you come clean or I walk." I was getting that queasy feeling in my gut.

"Honestly, Dr. Worth, that's it. She knows nothing about you, and nothing about us. Unless..."

"Unless, what?"

"Unless , well.. .the Governor directed that the project be located within the Board of Corrections so that an effective administrative apparatus will exist when the grants are awarded. The Governor has complete confidence in Ms. Reed-Wilder's ability, but he couldn't tell her anything because he doesn't know. I'm sure no one has told him anything."

"Jessup, for some reason you don't instill me with much confidence. Why didn't you warn me about Ms. Reed-Wilder?"

"I just didn't think it would be a problem. She's been with the Governor a long time. She's..."

"She's what?" I tried not to show too much surprise. "I thought she had been running the Board of Corrections for a long time."

"Oh, no. The Governor brought her with him when he took office in January. She was on his staff when he was mayor, his administrative assistant, I think. And, before that when he was DA, she was his special prosecutor."

"I see." Things were beginning to make more sense. I backed off Jessup. "Thanks for the call back, Jessup. I didn't mean to sound so angry. Her attitude and comments led me to believe that she knew more. Sorry, old boy."

"Don't call me here anymore unless it is a real emergency." Click went the phone.

Arrogant bastard. I shouldn't have backed off and let the little turd have the last word. Oh well, I'll use him just like he's using me.

I could understand Ms. Reed-Wilder's style and approach to people better now, knowing she possessed a prosecutor's mentality. What bothered me, however, was the Governor bringing her here and placing her in charge of the BOC. *Why not in some other capacity where her expertise could be more useful? He seems to have placed several people in key positions having to do with this grant money. I wondered how long the State's application for federal funding had been in the wind, and I wondered if Governor Osborne. ..no...you're reaching too far Matthew. Take it a step at a time.*

As I reflected longer, Carla's face flashed before me. *Oh, oh! Matthew, you might be on to something. There are connections here.* I picked up the phone and called her number. No answer. I called State Personnel. They had no such name listed. My imagination flamed my suspicions and created ideas that I didn't like. *Have you been set up again, Matthew? No I haven't. I'm letting my feelings take over. I'm not thinking. That's right, but you usually feel better than you think. I do not. I'm always rational at my work. Shut up.*

I looked up the Governor's office number and phoned. "Hello, Governor Osborne's office. May I help you?" She was very polite.

"Yes, I'm calling to reach Carla Renati and I don't have her extension. I understand she works for the Governor."

"Yes she does, sir. However, sir, right now she is with the Governor at a meeting in Los Angeles. May I transfer you to her voice mail?"

"When do you expect her back?"

"I don't know , sir, but the Governor will be back in his office on Wednesday. I can only assume the same would be true for Ms. Renati. If you would like to leave your number, I'll...."

"No thanks, it's not important, I'll call again later in the week. Thank you." I hung up. *Now what?*

Chapter 13

There was nothing further I could do now about Carla, so I decided to forget my suspicions for the moment, and find myself some coffee. Besides, I wanted to meet Jill to see what matched that charming voice and phone manner. I was surprised when I saw her sitting at the front desk. I had expected to see a young thirtyish-type in a mini-skirt and bouffant hair style. Instead, Jill turned out to be a sedate looking woman in her mid-forties, with grayish blond hair pulled neatly into a bun, and wearing a dark blue pleated skirt and long-sleeved camel-colored cotton blouse. Pure class all the way.

She turned when she heard me coming, and smiled. It was a warm natural smile that made me feel good, and immediately at ease. "Hello! You must be Dr. Worth. I'm Jill McCloud. Welcome to the BOC. It's going to be a pleasure having you here, I'm sure."

"Jill, it's my pleasure, and call me Matt, please. Dr. Worth is for the bureaucrats." She was a stunningly beautiful woman, with a high forehead, smooth complexion, sparkling blue eyes, a perky turned up nose, and a long regal neck. She wore a single strand gold necklace with one pearl that bobbed in and out of her milk-white cleavage.

"I'm afraid it will have to be Dr. Worth. We are not on first-name basis around here. You can call me Jill, but to those who work under you it is Dr. Worth. If you have any special requests, or if I can be of any assistance, please let me know."

"Thank you, Jill, I will." Her voice was soft and vibrant and she radiated a natural warmth of a woman who knew who she was and liked it.

"Right now, I could use some coffee."

"Oh, down at the end of the hall, the last door on your left. You'll find everything you need." Just then the phone rang, and she smiled and turned away.

As I walked down the hall, I heard voices coming from the coffee room. I entered and saw Ms. Reed-Wilder seated at the head of a long table flanked down the sides by six men and four women. They were drinking coffee and grabbing donuts off a large plate positioned in the center of the table.

They all looked up at me and paused in their motions and talk.

Ms. Reed-Wilder made the introductions. Three of the men were jail inspectors responsible for certifying that the county jails met the state mandated health and safety requirements. The other seven were corrections consultants who coordinated the state-funded training for all county probation officers and local jails and juvenile hall staff. Their faces and names were but a blur.

I'm not very good in new social situations and rarely remember a name after being introduced to a person. I needed a more personal association. However, I rarely saw any of these people again, because they were always out in the field working: a real dedicated group.

An air of stiff cordiality permeated the room for the next five minutes. Ms. Reed-Wilder smoothed out her napkin over and over between sips of coffee. When she drank, they drank. Suddenly, she looked at her watch, then rose and exited the room. It was 10:15 a.m. The others followed, each saying how nice it was to meet me as they walked out the door. Ten little solders all in a row.

I sat there sipping my coffee, contemplating the waste achieved by human conformity. In a few minutes I heard light footsteps gliding down the hall. Jill McCloud entered the room and smiled, "I see you found the coffee all right."

"Yes, thank you, but I'm afraid I interrupted the morning coffee ritual. Everyone left rather quickly after I came in."

"I wouldn't worry about that, Dr. Worth. Their time was up."

"Their time was up? You mean their coffee breaks are timed?"

"Oh yes. 10:00 to 10:15 a.m., and 3:00 to 3:15 p.m., whether they need it or not." Her sarcasm was obvious. "My time runs from 10:15 to 10:30 a.m. and from 3:15 to 3:30 p.m. A girl from the steno pool upstairs fills in for me on the phone while I'm away. Same for lunch, noon to 1:00 p.m.

"Jill, you don't impress me as the type to be regimented, and a moment ago you sounded critical of the structure here."

"You're right, in one sense, Dr. Worth. I don't like phony protocol, but I'm used to regimentation. My husband was a career officer in the air force, and we moved within a well-disciplined system for eighteen years." She was being direct and open, but her expression showed no hint of what she might be feeling.

"You say your husband was an officer. Is he no longer in the service?"

"He died three and a half years ago. He flew in the Diamond Four Squadron. They were performing in a centennial celebration in Utah, flying one hundred feet off the ground. One of the newer pilots turned the wrong way. Their wings touched, and they both crashed within seconds."

I put my hand onto hers. "I'm so sorry, Jill I didn't mean to pry. I..."

"It's all right, Dr. Worth. I haven't talked about it in a long time and I feel a sense of relief having told you. The hurt is still there, but at least he was doing what he liked. That's important. And, what we had was good. I have a lot of fine memories." Her voice cracked slightly and her eyes became moist.

We sat for what seemed like minutes, but knowing it was only seconds, looking into each other's face, then down at our hands together. "Well, now," she offered, forcing a lively tone back into her voice. "Let's have some more coffee before my time runs out." She got up and refilled our cups, regained her composure, and sat back down.

I felt as though we, as two strangers, had just shared a moment of intimacy. Her openness had exposed vulnerability and a capacity for love that stirred a longing deep within me and made me aware of my own loneliness. For the first time in four years I allowed myself to experience an emotional charge. And for some reason, Libby's face flashed before my eyes.

I directed the conversation back to my introduction to the rest of the staff at the coffee room. "You said that I shouldn't worry about their abrupt behavior, that their time ran out. I think it was more than that. You could have sliced the air into solid pieces. Do you know of any reason, Jill, why they would resent my being here?"

"I think it was the way in which the position was filled that has them worried. The gossip was flowing wildly last week before you arrived. With you coming in as a direct representative of the federal funding agency, some might think you're here to spy on them. Also, they thought one of them should have been appointed to the job on a permanent basis. Actually, Dr. Worth, I think it is the uncertainty of who you are and what you'll do here that upsets them. You've disturbed their safe little world. It might not be all you, though. I hear that things were much better before Ms. Reed-Wilder took over."

"I can imagine. But what about you, Jill? Are up upset?"

"No. A little curious, perhaps, but not upset." Her voice was soft and intimate once more. "I'm not included in the informal affairs around here. People come and go, and I just sit there and do my job." She looked at her watch, took one last sip of her coffee, and rose to leave, placing her hand on my arm as she did. "Thanks for sharing my coffee time, Matt. I enjoyed your company."

She left quickly and hurried back to her station. She had made her role here seem so simplistic, so cut and dried. And she had dropped the formality of Dr. and called me Matt, as she left the room. She seemed so forthright and friendly. But I had learned through the years that nothing is as it seems.

Back at my desk, I began sifting through the grant applications, trying to get a feel for the types of organizations and individuals who had applied. Garcia's application was on the top of the pile marked Northern California. As Jessup as said during our conversation at the motel, Garcia, along with two others had been given approval to find a location and to develop the initial stage of their community corrections plan in preparation for a final review.

Garcia was requesting an initial grant of $1.4 million to lease, remodel, and staff an abandoned warehouse in North Sacramento to house 150 inmates. This included an annual salary of $74,000 for himself. Some contact man I'm working with. He is going to double-dip at the public trough while the Feds run their little undercover scam.

The second application was from Robbins Nest, a newly formed non-profit corporation headed by James Robbins, a state parole agent working out of a Sacramento location. He wanted $46.7 million to establish five centers in the valley: Sacramento, Stockton, Tracy, Modesto, and Fresno, and another $7 million a year, over the next three years.

Robbins' proposal read well, but since the federal guidelines prohibited employees of any public agency from receiving funds, I would have to reject his application. And, besides, I couldn't justify having two centers located in Sacramento, and I had to assure that Garcia's grant was approved.

I picked up the phone and buzzed Jill at the front desk.

" Yes, Dr. Worth?"

"Jill, will you phone James Robbins at the State Parole office for me?"

"I'm sorry, Dr. Worth. I'm not allowed to make out calls for anyone. It ties me up in case of an in-coming call. You can reach an outside line by dialing 9." She sounded apologetic.

"O.K., thanks." I wouldn't want her to violate any of the Dragon Lady's policies. That was the new name I had just given Ms. Reed-Wilder: a name I'd heard used before by others facing similar personalities.

I looked up the phone number of State Parole and called. The receptionist said that Mr. Robbins was *out in the field*, a euphemism that often meant screwing off somewhere away from the office. I convinced her that my call was important, and she finally confided that he was probably out at the Miranda Inn over-seeing it's re-modeling for a correctional center.

Very interesting, I thought. He just barely submitted his application, and he must have known from the guidelines that he couldn't qualify. I decided to pay him a personal visit first thing tomorrow morning to clarify our position. I spent the rest of the day reviewing the other grant applications and making phone contact to verify various kinds of information they contained in support of their requests.

It was a boring day, having to deal with paperwork when I would much rather be dealing with people. I ended my day early and went home.

Chapter 14

I checked into the office the next morning, grabbed the car keys and gas credit card from my desk, and told Jill I was going *out into the field.* I located my issued car, a 2010 Ford Fusion, exited the parking garage, and headed east on the old Highway 50, which was called Capitol Avenue for about five miles, then the name changed to Folsom Boulevard.

Once I drove out of Sacramento proper, toward Rancho Miranda, the road was flanked on both sides by a series of look-a-like tracts constructed during the 1960's and 1970's to meet the population growth of Mather Air Force Base, a SAC base, and Aerojet General Corporation, a major government supplier of jet engines. Mather was still in business, but Aerojet had been reduced to a skeleton of its original size by changes in political administrations. After the assassination of President Kennedy, a number of government defense contracts were pulled out of California and shifted to Texas and other southern states.

Rancho Miranda had changed from a thriving suburban community of 30,000 middle class upward mobile families to a cheap rent area of east Sacramento, populated primarily by transient air force personnel and low income families. The Miranda Inn had been the after-hours favorite of

Aerojet executives, government bureaucrats, and air force officers. It looked now as if it had been abandoned for years. The windows on the bar and dining room were boarded up, the signs were down, and the motel area was bleak and deserted. The small shopping center behind it was beginning to take on the same appearance.

I parked behind what had been the motel office and walked over to the pool and lanai area. The lawn was full of weeds, but it had been mowed recently. The decking around the pool was badly cracked, and the pool itself was caked with dried green algae and fungus.

I heard a motel room door creak, and turned to see four big bad-looking men walking toward me. They wore paint spattered jeans and cut off tee-shirts, and their bulging muscles glistened with sweat. Two were black, one was white, and the fourth was Mexican.

"Well, a regular international welcoming committee, how thoughtful," I said.

"This place is closed, can't you tell," barked the Mexican.

"I'm not here to make reservations."

"What do you want, man?" asked the larger of the two Blacks. He was huge, with a round thick, ugly face, no neck and wide shoulders. He towered over the others. He looked mean. The other black was tall, but slightly built, and gangly, and he wore a diamond stud in his left ear lobe. He looked familiar. I'd seen him somewhere recently.

"I came to see James Robbins."

"What about?" demanded the white guy.

"Are you James Robbins?"

"No. What do you want with Robbins?"

"If you're not him, then I didn't come to see you, did I?" I rejoined, trying to sound just as firm as they did. By now the four had formed a semicircle around me and were standing only three feet away. I hated it when people got in my space, and I didn't like the odds.

"Sammy asked you a question, man. What do you want with Robbins?" asked the large Black, placing his hand on my shoulder and turning me toward him. All four were standing with their feet apart and their muscles were tightening as if preparing for the kill.

"I'm Jim Robbins," a voice called down from the second story balcony right above us. "What can I do for ya'?"

I looked up and saw a lean-faced man wearing a smirk on his pinkish colored face which was topped with thick carrot colored hair. I don't know how long he had been standing there, but he seemed amused by my obvious predicament.

"Send these four animals back to their kennels for some raw meat, and I'll tell you." I expected a fist in the back of my head any second.

" It's all right, boys. Get back to work. I'll handle this." The four backed away a few feet, then turned and walked slowly back to the room from where they had come. Their faces shared the expression of disappointment at being denied the right to tear off my head.

"Now, mister, like I said, what can I do for ya'?"

"I'm Dr. Matthew Worth, consultant to the Board of Corrections. I came to talk to you about your grant request."

He stood erect, looked surprised, then annoyed, and then he smiled and leaned over the railing. "Why sure, Dr. Worth, I'll be right down. Meet ya' at the corner, there." He pointed toward the stairs at the street end of the room complex. His voice became mellow and pleasant, and I figured I was in for a *good ol' boy* routine. He took firm, quick strides down the balcony and his western styled boots clanked loudly on the metal staircase as he took two stairs at a time.

"So you're Dr. Matthew Worth, huh?" He held out a small freckle-covered hand that gripped mine like a vice. "I heard ya' was on the job. Mighty pleased that you stopped by."

He was lean and wiry, and stood about 5' 7" in his boots. He wore neatly creased blue Wrangler jeans, a flowery western style shirt, and snake skin cowboy boots, with extra high heels.

"Mr. Robbins." I acknowledged his greeting. "Some welcoming committee you have there. Do you always have people greeted that way?"

"Don't mind them. They're just leery of strangers and protective of me. They're cons, ya' know, haven't learned their social graces yet. They meant no harm."

"I'll bet, especially that one huge Black. He looked as though he wanted to tear my head off just for the practice."

"That's Monroe. He does look mean, don't he. And, he can be, if I want him to be, or if he gets mad at you. Anyway, no harm, no foul."

"Right, no harm done. Where can we talk?"

"Come on in here, son, this here's my office for now 'til we get this place fixed up."

The appearance of his office was in sharp contrast with the rest of the motel: freshly painted walls and ceilings, a new queen sized bed and dresser, with matching night stands, all in heavy dark oak, two matching lounge chairs with floral print upholstery, and a new 37" Samsung HD television. He walked nimbly around behind a large oak desk in the corner, plopped himself on a thickly cushioned captain's chair, and put his feet up on the corner of the desk.

He observed me looking around the room. "Nice, huh?"

"Not bad," I said. "Are all the rooms like this?"

"Naw, this is the only one so far, but give us the final approval and we'll have this here place lookin' like new quicker than a horse can swat a blowfly."

I could not believe this guy was for real. I was beginning to doubt that I had the right Jim Robbins, state parole agent.

He pulled out a box of *Player Navy Cut* cigarettes and offered me one. "No thanks."

"Well, tell me Dr. Worth, what is it about my grant application that would cause you to drive all the way out here in this heat?"

"I'll come right to the point, Mr. Robbins. The federal guidelines prohibit any public employee from receiving these funds and/or running a funded program. You're excluded. As a state parole agent, you can't qualify."

His wry expression didn't change, but his little green eyes were dancing in thought. "Well, I'll tell ya', Worth. Don't you be bothering yourself over me. I ain't gonna' be gettin' the money, Robbins Nest will. It's a nonprofit corporation duly registered with the Secretary of State."

"You have this place licensed already? I know that you have been given the O.K. to prepare a preliminary plan and find a location, but you're a little premature in your planning." His expression still didn't change. I had expected a more vocal reaction, but he seemed calm and unconcerned, as if he thought he already had approval.

"Let me show ya' around, Worth. I think you'll agree we're gonna have a first class operation here." He started to rise, but I raised my hand like a stop sign.

"Let's not side step the issue, Mr. Robbins. Whether you want the money or a corporation you direct wants the money, the same guidelines apply. I don't see how we can qualify you."

"I guess you didn't read my application good enough. As soon as we get the go-ahead on the grant, I'm takin' a leave of absence from parole. And, I think if you read the guidelines again, you'll see that as long as I'm not drawing public pay, I can qualify." His lips curled up in a satisfied smile, and his green eyes twinkled with delight. He reminded me of a poker player whose hand I once called, thinking he was bluffing, and he laid down aces full.

"You might be right, Mr. Robbins, you might be right. I'll check into it more completely." He had caught me unprepared. Now I had to think of some other way to remove him from competing with Garcia.

I continued, "There is one other consideration, however. We've already considered qualifying another applicant for Sacramento, and I doubt that the area can support two centers."

"According to my information, the selections ain't gonna' be made for a several weeks yet. What da' ya' mean you're qualifying someone else?"

"Well, Mr. Robbins, the final grant recipients haven't actually been selected yet. I just meant that we liked the proposal of another applicant. It's very cost effective, and we'll have to weigh the merits of your program very carefully."

"Who's the other applicant?"

"I'm not at liberty to disclose any names."

"Probably that Mex, Garcia." All of a sudden Robbins' demeanor changed, and he looked mean and angry.

"I told you, I'm not at liberty to say."

"Listen, Worth." He took his feet off the desk and leaned forward, his eyes burning holes right through me. We got the best dang program anyone can offer. We got 250 rooms here, and a restaurant, plus a dozen store fronts in that abandoned shopping area next door. We're gonna' have 150 rooms for the parolees and a hundred rooms to rent out. Everyone's gonna' have a job, either in the motel, the restaurant, or in one of the shops we're gonna' open. We got it all, Dr. Worth, and when we get this off the ground, we're gonna' open a dozen more in the Bakersfield and Modesto areas. We're gonna' be self supportin' within the three year grant period. We meet the intent of the guidelines to a tee. And we got the same setup in the other four towns." As he talked, his manner became subdued and almost pleasant again.

He was right and he knew it. In fact, I was beginning to wish my job was legitimate because he seemed to have thought of everything needed by a parolee to make that transition back into the real world successfully. I decided that I had better change my tack.

"Sounds interesting, Mr. Robbins. Why don't you show me around the place now so I can see for myself?"

We toured the motel, with him talking in that cornpone style of his the entire time. I took comfort in the fact that he wasn't going to ask me to invest before I left.

The Inn was structurally sound and Robbins' ideas for remodeling and decorating were well thought out. I was beginning to like Robbins, himself. He had a certain appeal that was growing on me. Damn, just when I thought I had identified one of the bad guys, too. Well, he still might be one. I've been conned too many times to trust what anyone tells me, or to go with my first impressions. I told him I would continue considering both proposals, but that I didn't think there was room for two programs in the same area.

I mulled over Robbins' proposal on the drive back toward the office. I was beginning to get that queasy feeling; he looked too good. If it was a set-up, he could control the fund money in the entire valley; in fact, in most of northern California. I decided to contact Garcia and have him check out Robbins, while I ran the names of the staff he identified on his proposal through the state's criminal identification division, for any prior records.

Chapter 15

I drove back down Folsom Boulevard until I came to one of those freeway food places. I entered, stared at the menu, even though I already knew what I was going to have, then ordered a double cheeseburger, fries and a lime drink. While waiting for my order, I used my cell phone to call Garcia.

"Hello."

"Mr. Garcia, please."

"This is Garcia, who's this?"

"It's Worth, Matt Worth"

"Hey, baby, how you making it?"

"We have a possible problem."

"Like what, baby?"

"I just met with a guy named James Robbins at a site he's remodeling for a correctional center in Rancho Miranda. He's a state parole agent, but plans to take a leave to run the program if he gets the grant. He has four parolees working on an old motel with 250 rooms, plus a shopping center with twelve stores next door. Looks good. He's acting like he already has approval. Seems to know about you, too."

"No sweat, baby. Couldn't be better, in fact.," said Garcia. "I got the skinny on Robbins already. I have six parolees helping me out here to convert this old warehouse into dorms and rooms. MacClanahan arranged to have them sent to me from Folsom Prison. He also sent me a parolee who works for him. Name's Abner. He's my contact with MacClanahan. Abner just learned from one of the other cons that Robbins runs a burglary and fencing operation, and some narcotics distribution, with a dozen of his parolees. Robbins covers for them with the police and even tips them off to any raids or sting setups.

"Damn," I blurted. "I knew Robbins's plans were too good to be true."

"That's O.K., baby. Now we know what kind of guy he is. This might make our job easier."

The situation was developing fast. I wanted Robbins to get the grant award and start his programs so that we could follow where the money trail would take us. He might be alone in this, and we could wrap up the investigation quickly, as soon as we caught Robbins and some of the prison gang leaders doing something illegal with the money. Maybe Robbins was fronting for others who were actually running things. That might come out soon too, if Robbins got the grant award. However, if Robbins got the award, Garcia might not. I could justify having both centers if I worded it right.

"I'll have to make sure that both you and Robbins receive approval of your proposals."

"Don't sweat it, baby," said Garcia again. "They got so many parolees coming out of Folsom and Tracy that you could fund the entire Motel 6 chain to house them and still not have enough space. Fund us both and let's get rolling."

"OK. I'll be in touch."

"Keep cool, baby."

I stopped back at my office and put the other grant applications in my briefcase to take home for review. The atmosphere here was too stifling. On the way out the door, I told Jill I was going *out into the field* for the rest of the day.

She smiled knowingly. I felt a warm flush came over me as I looked at her. She radiated that natural open warmth, yet there was a detachment present, an assurance that no one could really get close. One of these days I'll have to find out what's inside there; who she is.

Chapter 16

Back at my apartment, I unlocked and opened the door cautiously, expecting to find something, but not knowing what it might be. Everything was secure and undisturbed, and no one was there. I didn't know whether to be pleased or worried. I changed into swimming trunks, poured some *Cuervo* over ice in a plastic glass, and went out to the pool.

I placed my drink on a lounge table and tossed my towel on the chair, then entered the pool. The water was cold and clean against the sticky afternoon valley heat. I dove deep and swam around under water until I thought my lungs would burst, and then leaped from the bottom of the pool, knifing through the surface. It felt great. Then I coughed and gasped for air. *Great shape, huh.*

I rolled out of the water onto the hot concrete decking and lay there absorbing the heat through by stomach, sweating out my back. I must have dozed off because I was suddenly jerked back into the present by the sound of a splash and the feel of cold water drops on my back. Then I felt something cold and wet brushing across my face. I opened my eyes and was greeted by the cold nose of a small fox terrier. When I blinked and rose up on my elbow, it yipped in my face and ran around getting excited, as only those little dogs can do, and it pissed all over the decking.

My first instinct was to toss it into the pool, but I saw that the source of the splashing was the old couple from No. 4 who I had disturbed the other night, looking for Carla. They were both portly and pale white, with chubby little round faces.

"Here, Pookie," the lady called. "Don't do that, now, you come to mamma."

I stood up and the dog began yipping again.

"Now Pookie, you stop that. That nice man won't hurt you." She picked up the dog and cradled it in her arms. Little did she know that had the dog been out here alone, he would have been swimming laps by now, under water.

She gave me a sullen look, then said, "Say, aren't you the one who knocked on our door the other night looking for some girl?"

"Yes Ma'am. Sorry about that. I had the wrong apartment." I tried to sound polite and apologetic.

"Well, you shouldn't go around disturbing people at all hours. We didn't know what to think."

"I know, Ma'am. Like I said, I'm sorry," and I picked up my towel and drink and walked back my apartment. Why was I being so polite? I had that feeling as though I should apologize even though I had done nothing wrong.

That's the feeling young people get around older people when they are scolded. Does that feeling ever stop? Oh well, I couldn't be rude, either.

I glanced at my watch and saw that it was after 6:00 p.m. My nap by the pool was longer than I thought. My mind was on Carla now. What is she doing in Los Angeles? What is she to Governor Osborne? She must fit into all this, but where? I checked my watch again as I considered my own questions. Hum, time for a drink.

I opened the sliding patio door and entered my apartment and poured some more *Cuervo* over ice, and sipped. *Ah!* Then I decided, at least for the time being, that Carla knew nothing.

The phone rang. It was MacClanahan. "Worth, we got trouble. I have a parolee planted with Robbins on the motel restoration job. You met him once, at the wharf. Willie, the tall, lean kid with diamond earrings."

"Oh, yes," I made the connection now. He was the one I recognized at Robbins' motel. "What's up Mac? What sort of trouble?"

"Willie phoned and said that Robbins blew his top after your visit. He was ranting about maybe not getting funded because of some Mex named Garcia, who had a proposal you liked better. Said the two of you could screw up his whole deal. Mumbled something about having to put a knife in your toaster too, and ice Garcia with something."

"That says it, Mac. Robbins is our man. No doubt about it. Son-of-a-bitch killed Dick James, too. I knew that the knife-in-the-toaster story was a phony."

"You're right Worth," agreed MacClanahan, "But what have we got? I've known Robbins for over twenty years. He's two-bit. He doesn't have the brains to put this together, or the balls to carry it off. No, Worth, Robbins is just a front man. Willie says that the cons trust Robbins. That's probably why they picked him."

"Who are *they* Mac?"

"I don't know, Worth, that's up to you to find out and tell us."

"Right, " I muttered. I knew MacClanahan was right, but I found it difficult to hold back. I wanted to run and nail Robbins for killing James. "What about James, Mac? Robbins must have been the one who killed him." I was sounding emotional again.

"I know, Worth, but now is not the time to deal with that." MacClanahan's voice was low, but firm. He sounded so composed about it all. Then it hit me, and I yelled over the phone, "You knew, Mac, all the time, you knew, didn't you?"

"Knew what, Worth?" MacClanahan's voice remained calm, but there was a note of caution in it.

"You knew that Robbins killed Dick James from the start. You must have, with your network of informants."

"Man, listen to me." MacClanahan's tone tried to reassure me, but I knew what he was going to say.

"Damn it, Mac, you knew, didn't you?" I demanded to know.

There was a long pause, then in a gravely whisper, MacClanahan said, "Yes, Worth, we knew. Willie was outside James' apartment when it happened. Robbins told him he was going in just to talk to James. He took Monroe in with him. You know Monroe. He was the other black guy, the great big one you saw when you went to the motel to meet Robbins. Apparently, they gagged James and rolled him up in a rug in which Monroe had cut a small hole to allow James' hand to stick out. They put a knife in his hand, stuck it in the toaster, then plugged it in. Afterwards, they unrolled James, and put the knife and toaster in the right positions to look like an accident."

"How does Willie know all this if he was outside?" I interrupted.

"Robbins called him in to help Monroe unroll James

and set it up. He was too late to help James," MacClanahan added, in an apologetic tone.

"Would he have helped if he could?" I retorted.

There was another pause. "No, Worth, probably not. He is under orders not to tip his cover"

"No matter what, Mac. No matter what the cost." I meant it as an observation, not a question. "What sort of game are we playing here, Mac? Why weren't you straight with me in the beginning?"

"I wanted to, believe me, Worth, but Holden is running this show and he was afraid of a leak if we told you."

"What about me, Mac? What is Willie going to do when Robbins has Monroe roll me up in a blanket?" I was sounding indignant and melodramatic now and I knew it. I wasn't naive. I knew there were risks and dangers when I took the job. It was just that once in a while when I am confronted directly with the values inherent in these cloak and dagger situations, I get pissed. They probably told Dick James less about the job than they told me, and he was naive.

"Come on, Worth. That's not fair and you know it," growled MacClanahan.

"I don't mean to blame you for this, Mac. I'm just frustrated that I can't do anything."

"But you can, Worth, you can. You can find out who is behind all this and why, and help us nail them all."

"Right, Mac." I was composed now and thinking again. "Did you warn Garcia?"

"I sent Abner over to tell him and to give him some cover if he needs it, but I don't think Robbins will do anything without orders. Like I said, he's just a front man, and he's not going to jeopardize his own position."

"I hope you're right. Thanks for the call, Mac. Sorry that I got hot there. And, I think I can find a way to fund both Robbins and Garcia, so Robbins shouldn't feel threatened. Keep in touch."

Chapter 17

I hung up the phone and reached for my drink. All the ice had melted. I took a swallow, but it was flat. I poured in some more *Cuervo* without adding ice. That is one thing I liked about this brand. I could drink it cold or warm, with or without ice, and it always tasted good. I took another swallow and chewed a mouthful as it went down.

I looked at the pile of grant applications in my briefcase, which was lying open on the coffee table. Garcia's application was still on top. I thought about what MacClanahan had said about Robbins not doing anything without orders. Mac's probably right. Probably... I didn't like the sound of such a tentative concept in a situation like this. And, we don't know what orders Robbins might or might not have. He seemed very impulsive to me.

I copied down the address of the warehouse that Garcia had listed on his application and looked up the street in my Thomas Brothers map book. It was in the north area, west of the freeway, just off Arden Way. I didn't know for sure that Garcia was there, but I thought I should find out.

I slipped on a shoulder holster fitted for my Mateba .357, then shoved my Colt .380 into an inside-the-pants clip-on holster that I wore on my inside right hip. I felt like a gunfighter getting ready to walk out into the street for a show-down. *Who knows*, I mused, *maybe I am.*

I put my *Cuervo* on the counter without drinking any more. My concealed weapons permit is automatically void if I am under the influence of alcohol, and I didn't want to chance being pulled over for some traffic offense and have some city cop get curious.

I drove north out of downtown, on what used to be Highway 80 until it picked up the freeway, then exited off onto Arden Way and turned left under the freeway to the second stop sign. It was the heart of a light industrial and warehouse district. Wilson Street. I turned right two blocks to Bryan, and then left to 1193. This was it, a large two story warehouse with corrugated siding and roof, and a sliding front entry door large enough to drive a truck through.

There was a small glassed-in office area in the front, with a regular entry door. I parked in front, got out, and peered through the office window. There was a dim light on somewhere back in the warehouse area, but no sign of a light anywhere else. A cigarette butt was lying beside the door.

I picked up the cigarette; it was a *Players*. Damn!

I tried the office door. It was unlocked. I eased the .357 out of its holster, held it down at my side and entered the office. An old wooden desk and chair, and a metal filing cabinet were all that was there. The door from the office to the warehouse area was already open. I walked slowly into the warehouse toward the dim light that seemed to be hanging from the ceiling at the rear of the building.

The center of the warehouse was bare, but there were rows of shelves on three sides. The ceiling was 12 or 15 feet high, and I could see stairs leading up to the second story at the far end. As I got closer, I could see that the light was actually coming down from the second story through the stair well, rather than from a hanging light.

Someone must be up there, I thought. I wanted to call out Garcia's name, but I swallowed the word. Now was not the time to announce my presence. I thought I heard a movement behind one of the rows of shelves on my left. I stopped walking, and I think my heart stopped too. I listened carefully. Nothing.

I stepped out again toward the stairs until I reached the bottom step. It was so quiet that I could hear my heart pounding now against my breast bone. A shiver started at the base of my skull and swirled down my spine. I changed gun hands just long enough to wipe off the sweaty palm, and then started up the stairs.

There were twelve stairs. They were tall. The third one squeaked. I froze. No sound anywhere. Stepped again. As I reached the top, I bent over until I was ready to move up into the second story. Then, I sprang up and jumped into the room. With my .357 held two handed, I began a quick 270° spin toward the light. I didn't get far.

At the far end of the room, just behind where the ceiling light was glaring, was the body of a man hanging from the rafters. His neck was jammed into the convergence of a rafter and two support beams. The body cast a giant shadow onto the wall behind. It was grotesque; surreal. It was Garcia.

I didn't move. There was someone else in the room. I sensed him. I didn't hear anything or see anything, but he was there. The hair on my neck was standing straight out. These are the times when I stop thinking and let my feelings take over. They are seldom wrong.

There were a number of old wooden egg crates piled up neared the corner on my right, but there was a space to get around behind them. I moved ever so slowly to within ten feet of the crates, both hands supporting my .357. Not a sound, but he was there. "I'm going to count to three, then shoot 15 rounds into these crates," I called out in my boldest voice.

"One two..."

"Oh, mon, it's you, Worth," came a voice from behind the crates. A huge black body emerged from the dark corner.

"You scared the shit out of me, mon." he said. "I thought it was one of them coming back"

It was Abner. He was wearing jeans, a blue denim shirt, black tennis shoes, and a red bandana tied around his bald head. I was pointing the *Mateba* right at his stomach. I swear that I had the trigger pulled halfway. I relaxed my finger and pointed the gun to the floor.

"Abner. You remember me?"

"Sure, mon. Mr. Mac say to look out for you and Mr. Garcia; to take care of you two."

We both looked up at Garcia hanging in the rafters. "What happened, Abner? Mac said he sent you over to warn Garcia."

"I got here too late, mon. I see three men leaving, as I come here. They get into a big Lincoln with a tire on back and big cow horns on front of hood. I wait 'til they leave, then I go in. I find Mr. Garcia up there just like you did, mon. But, before I can get him down, I hear a car stop in front, then the office door open. I think it be the three men coming back, so I hide in the corner. I wait there long time, mon. You sneak good. I hear you squeak once on the stairs, but I didn't know you here 'til you holler out you gonna shoot."

Abner was sweating and breathing hard just like I was. I guess it doesn't matter how big a person is, fear strikes a common cord. And, adrenaline courses through a body the same, regardless of its size.

"It's all right, Abner. I guess we both got here a little too late."

"You know who do this, mon?"

"I think so, Abner. It had to be Robbins, with the car you described. I've never seen his car, but he's the only person I know who would have the taste to put steer horns on his car hood, and the gall to drive it here where he commits murder."

"I don't think Robbins big enough to get Mr. Garcia, mon. He's just a little squeak."

"You're right, Abner. When I say it was Robbins, I mean he gave the order, Monroe did the job."

"Monroe, huh. He's a bad man, Mr. Worth. He's evil."

"You know Monroe, Abner?"

"Oh yes, mon. We be together in the same cell block for a year at Folsom. One day I see him kill a snitch in the day room. He gagged him, turned up the TV, two guys hold him down, then Monroe shove a broom handle two feet inside him up his ass. Then, they let him up to try and get help. He took two steps, pulled his gag and screamed. Loud, mon. I never heard a scream that loud, ever. The guard blew his whistle to get help, but the snitch screamed for minutes, mon., waiting, and then he die. I looked at Monroe. He's grinning, then he gets a look on his face that I thought he come in his pants. Then he relaxes and watches TV, while the guards tried to find out what happened."

"I know how it is in a situation like that, no one knows anything."

"That's right, mon. Monroe, he had a reputation then. Nobody mess with him. He's evil. He likes to hurt people bad and he don't even feel about it. He is good with bombs too, I hear. He likes to blow up cars and people."

"We better get out of here, Abner. Much as I'd like to take Garcia down, we have to leave the evidence as it is for the police. And, we can't be found here because we could never explain it. I'll call the police from a pay phone, and then drop you off wherever you want. You call MacClanahan and tell him what happened. I have to think this out. Tell him I'll be in touch."

I drove back down Arden Way toward the Country Club Shopping Center for about ten blocks, before I spotted a pay phone in front of a *7-11* store. I didn't dare use my cell phone. I phoned the police on the regular number rather than 9-1-1 so they could not trace the call. I gave dispatch the address and told her to have an officer check upstairs for a body. I also suggested that she call a coroner's investigator in on it too, then hung up. Garcia deserved better, but like MacClanahan said, *Now is not the time to deal with that.*

When I got back to the car, Abner was gone. I knew he could find his way wherever, and that he would contact MacClanahan, so I wasn't worried, at least not about him. I drove slowly back to my apartment, sorting out all the events that had occurred so far, and trying to get a handle on where to go next.

Chapter 18

When I put the key in the lock of my apartment door, it was unlocked. I turned the handle and slowly pushed the door open, pulling out my Mateba and leveling it toward the opening as I did. As I entered, I saw Carla sitting cross-legged on the couch reading one of my Elmore Leonard novels. She looked up, started to smile, and then jerked her body against the back of the couch. Her eyes stared at my gun for a moment, then she relaxed, smiled again and said, "Well, Matt, darling, do you always make such a grand entrance into your own apartment?"

Her tone sounded forced, as if she was deliberately trying to joke about something serious. I walked toward her, gave a long look in the kitchen area, then into my bedroom as I passed the door. The gun was still leveled. She looked at it again, as I approached her. I gave the room a sweeping look, checked the sliding door to the patio, then turned back to her, smiled, and laid the gun on the coffee table.

"Hi, Carla. I'm surprised to find you here," I said, sounding friendly and casual. I was trying to determine how to play this out.

She got up, walked to me and put her arms around my neck. Now she looked serious again. "Matt, what is it ? What's going on? Why the gun?"

She was looking me right in the eye and her concern was evident. *Damn it. How much can I tell her? Does she know anything? Is she in this too?* A hundred thoughts raced across my mind, like subliminal advertising on TV, while I calculated how to proceed. I decided to play it down as nothing, and then switch the focus back to her role with the Governor.

I looked her in the eye right back, smiled warmly, and said, "It's nothing, Carla. I've had a couple of crank calls while you were gone and someone broke into my apartment the day I arrived. They searched through my effects, but nothing was missing. I'm just overly cautious, I guess. I had my gun with me today because I went to the police firing range to practice this afternoon."

She gave me a questioning look.

"I'm not a gun nut," I continued, "but I was raised with guns and I enjoy target shooting. This one is new. I picked up the *Mateba* off the table and held it casually in my hand. I haven't got the feel of it yet, so I played hooky this afternoon and went to the range to practice."

"When I found my door unlocked just now I got a little paranoid, I guess. I came in thinking I was going to catch someone in the act."

She looked satisfied, and then looked toward the gun. I looked at the gun as well. "I better put this away where it belongs." As I walked into my bedroom, I realized how easily I had lied. And so well, I thought. I took off my jacket, tossed it on the bed, slipped off the shoulder holster, and stored it and the .357 in the dresser drawer. However, I pulled the clip-on holster free from my belt and moved it around to my left hip. I decided to keep the Colt .380 on my person until this job was over and I was back home in Oak Grove.

"How about a drink, Carla?" I was back into my warm intimate voice.

"Sure, Matt. Scotch, if you have it. Make it light, will you."

"I missed you. I called you at work Monday, but the secretary said you were in Los Angeles with the Governor." I tried to sound matter-of-fact and not questioning in tone.

"I missed you too, Matt, but duty called and I didn't have a chance to let you know I was going."

I made her a tall, light scotch. *Dewar's* was my house brand, poured myself about four ounces of *Cuervo* over cracked ice, and carried them into the living room. "Here you are, Carla."

We both took a healthy swallow. "What was the duty this time?" I tried to sound interested and not suspicious.

"Well, as you know, I work for Governor Osborne. He had to attend a fund raiser in Los Angeles and wanted me to go with him so I could help him with any speech he might have to give. I just had time to rush home, pack an overnight bag, and get to the airport."

She took another swallow of her scotch. "That tastes great, Matt, thanks." She tucked her feet under her cheeks and snuggled into the corner of the couch and pulled the corner pillow into her lap.

I gave her my best sure-I-know smile, and said, "Overnight with the Governor, huh? Sounds hinky to me." She picked up another pillow off the couch and threw it at me.

"You men," she said, laughing. "You know it's not like that." I caught the pillow, sat down in the chair across the coffee table from her, and threw it harmlessly back on the couch. "I'm the Governor's speech writer, and his appointment secretary, and I'll tell you truly, Matt, he wouldn't know whether to piss or offer a toast if I wasn't right there to tell him." We both laughed and took another swallow of our drinks.

"Fund raiser," I queried. "He's been elected and in office for six months. Why a fund raiser now?"

"Pay his campaign bills, I think. He ran up quite a large debt that the Committee covered for him, so he's helping to pay some of it back through personal appearance fund raisers."

"Un-huh," I mumbled. "Sounds boring."

"Not really," she responded. "The Vice- President was there to give the keynote speech."

"So?" I said.

"So, nothing," she sounded a little indignant.

"What's so great about seeing the Vice-President, especially the one we have now?" I thought I'd push her just to see how serious she was in her views.

"He's got a nice ass," she blurted, then laughed like a little kid who had just pulled a trick on a friend.

I don't think of myself as a shy person, or as a prude, but I'm not used to being around a woman who always acted out what she felt, and said what she thought. I felt as though I might be blushing, too, but I hoped it didn't show. "A nice ass, huh?" I grabbed the pillow from the couch and threw it at her. "Well he might have a nice shaped ass, but he has a marble sized brain."

We both laughed, as if we didn't know what other reaction to express, then took another swallow of our drinks.

"Actually, I don't know what the Vice-President was doing there. He said he was helping to raise funds for the Committee, but I think he was there to size up the governor as a presidential candidate in the next election. At least that is what the governor hopes. "

I often joked about the Vice-President's ambitions , but the thought of him actually working behind the scenes for another President scared me. He's dangerous. But enough of my petty concerns. I needed to learn as much from Carla as possible.

"What's the Committee, Carla? What's it all about?"

"Well", she replied in a serious tone, sitting upright and putting her drink down on the coffee table. "It's a political organization that backs certain candidates running for key positions in certain state or federal offices. It always seems to have plenty of money when it needs it, but it often holds these fund raisers, too."

"Maybe they aren't fund raisers, Carla. Maybe they're just image-building sessions. It's a good marketing tool, especially when you can draw big name speakers like the Vice-President and Governor." She looked puzzled. So did I.

"Who's behind the Committee?" I asked. "Who runs the day-to-day operation?"

"His name is Adair Zandi," she replied.

"Never heard of him," I said.

"I don't know much about him, Matt. I heard he landed in Los Angeles from somewhere in Eurasia six or seven years ago, with a suave personality, a classy wardrobe, and big money behind him. I don't know where the money comes from, but he immediately formed the Committee for Honest Government, and has since been backing winning candidates at every level of government."

"Did the Committee back Osborne for Mayor of Freeport?" I asked. I was getting excited now. I wasn't sure where this was going, but I had a feeling that it was in the right direction.

"Yes, I think so," she sounded sure, but looked uncertain.

"And, of course, it backed Osborne for Governor?"

"Of course," she acknowledged.

"Carla," my tone became more serious than I intended. "Did the Committee back the President and Vice-President in their last election?"

"I don't know, Matt, I don't know. There are no outward signs from either side."

"I wonder..." my voice trailed off into silence, while my mind flashed on several possible answers. "Are they going to back any particular candidates in the coming presidential election?"

"Hey, you." Her serious tone was gone and her expression was open, warm, and smiling again. "What's all this interest in politics? You became so serious all of a sudden. We better change the subject and change your attitude to something more useful." She gave me that come-hither look and patted the couch beside her.

I thought I could learn more from Carla, and I had that gnawing feeling that she was somehow involved in this mess. And, if she was, then maybe Osborne was, or visa-versa. I couldn't put it together yet. There were too many unconnected strings. However, it seemed obvious that she was through talking about politics, as she called it, and I might make her wary if I pushed the subject. There will be another time.

She patted the couch beside her again. I didn't feel like anything intimate now, and I didn't know if I could pretend well enough to convince her I was enjoying it if we did. Anyway, I got up, walked around the coffee table, sat down beside her, and put my arm around her neck. Her eyes scanned my face, and then settled on my mouth. Her lips were parted and wet.

She reached up, put her hand behind my head and pulled me down to her. Her kiss was full and long, and her tongue moved rapidly in and out and around my mouth. It felt good and she tasted better, yet I still didn't feel like anything intimate. I couldn't help but think of Garcia, and I saw him again, hanging from the rafters. I could visualize Monroe breaking his neck, then jamming it between the beams like that. The thought that she might be involved made it all the more horrible.

I pulled away from Carla slowly. "Sorry, Carla. It's been a long day and I have to get up early tomorrow." I looked a little sheepish. I didn't know what else to say.

"It's O.K., Matt. Not to worry. It's been a long day for me too." She picked up her glass, took a large swallow, put the glass back down, and turned to me and smiled. "Really, it's O.K."

She really seemed to understand, and yet there was nothing that she knew that she could understand. Or, maybe there was. Maybe she came around just to learn what I knew.

She was an enigma. I hoped for the best, but feared the worst, and really had no idea what to think. I picked up my *Cuervo* and swallowed what was left.

"Want another." I asked, gesturing with my empty glass.

"No thanks, Matt. It's time that I left. You better get some sleep. Call me," she said, and stood up and walked to the door, turned and waved once, blew a kiss, and left.

I watched the Tear-Drop cheeks snap back and forth as she walked out the door.

It was late and my head was so full of ideas that they kept running into each other. The *Cuervo* really didn't help matters, but I poured another half a glass anyway, took it into the bedroom, and set it on the night stand, stripped and crawled under the covers.

When I was first talked into this job at the motel meeting, MacClanahan said something about a new organization being formed that might be behind a conspiracy to get the grant funds. The name or initials ZORN was mentioned. It seemed too obvious to have figured that out so soon, but I laid out the names of the players we had so far: Osborne, Robbins, and N. Who could N be? And Z. Who could Z be? Who's left? Carla, Jessup, Ms. Reed-Wilder?

Nothing would fit. Robbins, yes, but Osborne? Not a governor. No one who's dirty could get this far in his political career without leaving a trail. Zandi? I needed to learn more about both him and Osborne.

I decided it was time to call in the expert, my own personal political encyclopedia and gossip sheet, Hatfield P. Gowdy. Don't know what the "P' stands for; he would never tell anyone.

Chapter 19

When I first met Hat in Nevada, he was not really inclined toward work. He wasn't lazy, actually, He was a rock-hound by nature and he just preferred being out in the hills, digging around for minerals; nothing valuable, just those in which he could find well-formed crystals. He would isolate the best ones and mount them on small black ink-stained corks. Micro-mounts, he called them. He would work in the mine just long enough to save a grubstake, and then he would head off into the hills, sometimes for weeks at a time.

He let me come with him one summer. When anyone asked him what he was looking for, he would reply, *old money*. He used to say that was the only kind worth having.

On one trip in 1985 he headed north on a dirt road out of Lovelock, in his 4-wheel drive GMC, through the remains of the ghost towns of Vernon and Seven Troughs, then northeast to an area called Rabbit Creek. He was digging in a tunnel that had been closed in the early mining years because of a cave-in, but which had been turned into a gully by unusually heavy rains the previous winter. He picked out a rock and there embedded in it was a gold nugget as big as a quarter. He picked around the spot for about an hour, and then hit a vein.

A rich deep vein, then he hit another. He knew that this was his *old money*. He immediately went to Carson City and checked the records. The old mining claims had long since been abandoned. He filed his own claim, and his Rabbit Creek Mining Company was in business.

New mining operations had sprung up all over Nevada in recent years because the new technologies and price of gold and silver made it profitable. Within two months, Hat had worked out a profit sharing arrangement with Alcancŏte Mining Corporation, a French company. They re-opened the mine, expanded the operation, and did the work, while Hat collected royalties and sat in the shade sipping whiskey.

I learned later that Hat helped out my mom financially after my dad died, and paid most of my tuition and board at UNR. I didn't see him for several years after I finished college, but we kept in contact by e-mail, and his image never left my mind. His six feet frame was lean and hard, with a face that looked like wrinkled leather, and pale blue eyes that sparkled like the crystals he mounted. He had a disarming smile and could be very charming when he wanted to, which wasn't often.

Hat didn't mix well with people, and when he did he usually presented an arrogant and unconcerned front until he had a chance to learn who they were and what they wanted.

He was the unique sort of person who didn't remind me of anyone else. Not many people passed through that facade to really know him. Fortunately, I did, and he knew me as well. We were friends.

Eight years ago, after my mom died, he moved to California, bought a cottage in the village of Inverness in northern Marin County, and emerged himself in studying photography, computers, and California politics, an odd combination that I never could understand. We have seen each other often since his move. He always said that we were the only family that he had, and now my sister and I were all that was left.

I found myself smiling fondly as I reflected on the past. I had spent as much time with Hat as I had with my folks, maybe even more during the summers when he'd let me go off rock hunting with him.. He bought me my own pick and rock-hunting vest and ....

Chapter 20

I awoke about 6:00 a.m. The night stand light was still on, and the half-filled glass of *Cuervo* was on the stand, where I had placed it last night. Obviously, I had fallen asleep in the middle of last night's reverie. Something I rarely do, lament about the past, that is.

As I became conscious of where I was, I felt a growing pressure on my bladder. That must have been what woke me up. Well, it's time to get up anyway. I got up and alleviated the pressure.

I heard the coffee pot begin to perk as I walked out of the bathroom. It was set on a timer. I slipped on a pair of shorts, walked into the kitchen, and poured a large glass of *V-8 juice*. I didn't feel much like breakfast. I considered making toast, but shuddered at the thought, and settled for a half a cold bagel with cream cheese.

The coffee was ready, and it had that real coffee smell. I filled a mug, carried it into the bathroom, where I gulped it down between shaving and a shower. After dressing, I went out into the kitchen again, poured another mug of coffee, and ate the other half of the bagel. Then, I looked up Hat's phone number and dialed.

It rang twice, then: "Hello, you have reached 428-1935. I'm not here to answer your call directly, but if you'll leave your name and number, I might call you back."

The voice was Hat's, all right, deep, rich and resonant, but I could tell from the inflections that it really was Hat and not his machine. He often answered that way just to screen calls.

"Hatfield, you old desert rat, it's me, Matt."

"Well, Matthew, my boy, where the hell are you, and why aren't you here?"

"I'm still in Sacramento, Hat, on that job." I filled him on all the details that had transpired thus far.

"Hat, I need to know about two politicians that you might have heard about."

"Tell me who, Matthew, and I'll do what I can, which undoubtedly will be a considerable amount."

"Governor Osborne and a man named Adair Zandi." As I spoke, I could hear Hat's computer warming up in the background. I marveled at how quickly he had embraced the modern world and all our technologies, as soon as that old money came his way.

"I'll call you back within the hour," replied Hat.

My cell phone rang fifty minutes later. It was Hat. "Let

me see, Matthew." He always began like that when he was going to demonstrate how much he knew. "Adair Zandi, age 49, arrived in Los Angeles seven years ago from Iran, by way New York. Sources say that he arrived in New York with a young Italian wife, the former Mariana Teresa Natalie. Her father is Carlo Natalie, a wealthy industrialist headquartered in Milan, Italy. Some rumor about mob ties, but nothing specific."

Hat took a deep breath and continued. "Osborne, let's see. He's 56, the youngest son of Judge Franklin Osborne of Los Angeles, raised in a military academy in Whittier, then on to Harvard Law School, where he flunked out during his second year. He returned to Los Angeles and graduated two years later from a local private law school that was heavily financed by his father. Then he joined the firm of Osborne, Cisneros, and Chance. Passed the Bar on the first time; hard to believe. Within a year, the firm opened a branch office for him in Freeport, south of Los Angeles. Fortunately for the firm, they also hired an office manager to run the day-to-day operation. Apparently, Osborne preferred the public limelight to the court room because he spent most of his time in civic and political affairs within the county.'

"Perhaps he liked the power that politics offered," I interjected.

"I don't think so, Matthew. Some people enter politics for dominance, some for prominence. Osborne craves the latter."

"O.K., Hat, please continue." I could tell that he didn't like the interruptions.

"Well, it wasn't long before the local district attorney announced his retirement. When he refused to support one of the contenders from within his office, it threw the door wide open. Osborne either hired, or was approached by the public relations firm of Lehey and Natalie to..."

"Wait a minute, Hat. Repeat that, the public relations firm of who?"

"Ah, paying attention are you. I thought you'd like that one. Yes, Matthew, the same Natalie family. This Natalie is Gaetano, the oldest one."

"Bless you Hatfield. Bless your nosey old soul. I see an image emerging here; let's develop it further"

"Well Matthew, I don't know by whom you expect me to be blessed, and I'm not sure I would like the process, but let me continue." His tone was the finest blend of arrogance and sarcasm that he could muster. "Anyway, Osborne ran for DA on his PR image, and his good looks and name. Have you ever seen him, Matthew?"

"No, I haven't Hat."

"He cuts a fine figure, really quite dashing. About 6'2", large frame, with John Wayne shoulders and walk, blond wavy hair with a touch of gray at the temples, a boyish smile for the older ladies, and an array of Italian suits that would make a movie wardrobe man jealous."

"I get the picture, Hatfield. On with the tale."

"Osborne won the election hands down. By coincidence, one would hope, a series of brutal crimes occurred within the first two years of the term. You might remember: the trailside murders, the killing and mutilation of those seven teenage girls on the jogging trail of Garth Park; the string of nine sexual assaults at Los Madonna's Beach; and the child molestations in that day care center by three trusted staff members."

"Yes, I remember, Hat." Actually, I had forgotten all about those because I read and hear about similar stories so often that they enter my brain quietly and slip unnoticed onto a storage tape marked brutal crimes. I recalled , now, that the press sensationalized all three incidents almost to the point of panic in the streets.

"I recall, now, that the press had a field day with those crimes." I offered my recollection to Hat to assure him that I knew what he was referring to.

"Yes, Matthew, the press also thought they could hang the DA's office out to dry for inactivity, but the police got lucky and caught all the suspects quickly, and for once seized all the evidence legally. The defense attorneys couldn't find any loopholes, and Osborne pushed for quick trials. The irony here is that Osborne had never tried a case in his life. Until these crimes came along, all the prosecutions were handled by either a regular deputy or by Osborne's special prosecutor, a Ms. Reed-Wilder, while he did the *office networking*, to use a phrase popular today."

Hat continued. "The defense attorneys viewed the evidence in all the cases as irrefutable, so they plea-bargained away their clients' chances to beat the rap at trial. Osborne had easy convictions, saved the county from a rampant crime wave, and the press had to laud him as a savior in order to get any story out of it. Shortly after that, about two years ago, the Committee began a campaign to nominate Osborne for Governor. No one else had a chance in the party because the Committee wouldn't back anyone else, and the stalwart party members put the squeeze on everyone else to fall into line. The opposition didn't have a chance either. They had six candidates all yelping at Osborne's heels, but they couldn't settle their differences and come out with a strong candidate.

Consequently, for them, mediocrity won out, and in the final election, the image of Osborne was too captivating for the public to pass up. He won by a landslide. Oddly enough, the opposition candidates easily won for Secretary of State and Attorney General. So there you have it, Matthew, the life and times of Adair Zandi and Governor Osborne in a nutshell."

"Wow, Hat. I'm impressed. You really outdid yourself on this one. How do you come by all this information anyway?"

"Research, my boy. Research, and proper connections. That's my stock in trade now, you know." His boasting tone took on more arrogance than sarcasm, but I could still hear an overlay of self-mockery that had always been a cornerstone of Hatfield P. Gowdy's foundation.

"Thanks, Hat. I owe you one. I'll call you soon and we'll do something. We'll make a day of it, like you suggested. And Hat, see if you can find out anything more about Zandi."

"You're on, my boy. Take care."

I hung up the phone, walked into the bedroom to get my coat and briefcase, and looked into the mirror. *Matt, old boy, this is getting interesting. By Jove, I think we're on to something. I'm not sure what, but something.*

Chapter 21

I drove to the office and decided to call MacClanahan first thing. I thought that we'd better move quickly on this before anyone else gets killed, especially if it's me. Also, with Garcia dead, I needed to clarify what my lines of communication would be.

I parked at the curb about a block from the office and, before getting out, I switched on the remote starter system. I carried the control start mechanism in by briefcase or pocket. I hadn't used this lately, but I had one of these remotes installed on every car I've owned since 2005. My partner at the time was blown up in his own car by a bomb planted the night before by the coke smuggler we had been after. I decided to use it regularly until this job was over.

Ms. Reed-Wilder met me by the switchboard as I entered. "How have you found the grant applications so far, Dr. Worth?" she asked in her most officious manner.

"Well, actually Ms. Reed-Wilder, I haven't completed them all. I still have three to study" In reality, I had read only one, the one belonging to Robbins. I knew I needed to read the others quickly, but it irritated me the way Ms. Reed-Wilder asked, assuming that I had read them all when she probably knew that I hadn't. I hated it when people played *Gotcha*.

"When might I receive a preliminary review of your findings?" she asked abruptly. "I want to go over them with you soon, so that we can initiate the funding process on schedule."

"I'll complete my preliminary study by 4:00 p.m. today. We can meet tomorrow morning, if you like". I could be as abrupt and cold as she.

"Fine, Dr. Worth. Let's say 9:00 a.m." She turned, walked back into her office, and closed the door.

I looked over at Jill, who had been sitting at the reception desk the entire time. I gave her a quick shudder to symbolize the cold effect of Ms. Reed-Wilder. She smiled and said good morning. That helped start the day.

"Good morning, Jill. I'll be in my office all day today, I think. Let me know if you go anywhere for lunch. I'd like you to pick up something for me, if you will."

"Certainly, Dr. Worth. I'll call you." As usual, her warm and supportive tone had a buoyant effect on my spirits.

I sat down at my desk, loosened my tie, placed the grant applications in front of me, and called MacClanahan's phone number.

"Hello," came the low whisky voice that I had come to recognize.

"Mac, this is Matt Worth." There was a pause.

"Is this a clean line, Worth?"

"I think so. It's my cell phone," I replied, taking on his hushed tone.

"Let's meet."

"Where?"

"Halfway. Do you know where the *Nut Tree* is, or was?"

"Sure," I replied. It was once a famous restaurant and tourist shopping mecca just outside the city of Vacaville, about halfway between Sacramento and San Francisco, but it had been closed now for several years.

"Across the highway is the Coffee Tree."

"Yes, I know that, too," I reassured him.

"Meet me there at 6:00 p.m. We'll talk." Click. The phone went dead.

I had an idea. I sorted through the business cards given to me by all those agents at the motel that morning and found the one for Robert J. Orneles, Special Investigator, State Department of Justice. Sounded impressive. MacClanahan didn't trust anyone, and I wasn't sure how much to trust him. I thought it was time to bring another party on board. I phoned Orneles' business number.

"Hello, you have reached the Office of the Department of Justice. If you know the extension of the person you are calling, you may press it now. If you are calling for consumer affairs, you may press 1 now. If you...." I pressed the extension number shown on the card.

Voice mail. When it first came out I resented it as another step in depersonalizing my world. However, after using it a few times, I realized how much more efficient it was than dealing with any live receptionists. They would ping-pong my calls around an entire office building without any purpose at all, and then disconnect me. This way, I at least had some control over where my call might go. Also, the voice mail doesn't have an attitude, if you know what I mean.

"Hello, this is Jean Bethal, secretary to Robert Orneles. May I assist you?"

I hung up quickly. I didn't think anyone should know I was calling. Maybe she logs in his calls. God, was I getting paranoid, or what? I hope that this overly suspicious behavior of mine was only an aberration inherent in the nature of the present situation. I looked again on the card Orneles had given me. He's penned in his cell number, but I'd missed it in my haste. I dialed it.

"Hello," he answered without identifying himself. "Who is this?" His tone was business-like and cautious.

"This is Worth." There was a pause. "Matt Worth, you know, the Nevada Kid."

"I know who you are, Dr. Worth. I'm not sure this is wise calling me here."

"Why, is your phone bugged, or is mine?"

"I don't know about yours, but mine is not, I can assure you, unless someone is smarter than I am. I check it regularly, and sweep the room daily."

"Wow! And I thought I was paranoid."

"Save the remarks, Worth. Why did you call?"

"Did you hear about Garcia?"

"No. What about him?"

I told him about Garcia, and summarized what I had learned about Robbins. "Things are moving fast, Orneles, and I'm afraid that it's all going to turn to shit unless we act soon."

"Jesus...." he reacted. "I don't think we expected anything overt at this point. Maybe Robbins acted on his own without consulting higher-ups."

"MacClanahan doesn't think so," I countered. "Thinks he's a front man just doing as he's told."

"Perhaps," Orneles acknowledged. "Either way I agree that we need to move on this now, but in what direction? That's the rub."

"MacClanahan and I are meeting tonight to process what we have, and decide how to do just that. Want to be there?"

"Absolutely! Where?"

"At the Coffee Tree near Vacaville."

"I know the place. What time?"

"At 6:00 p.m. And, Orneles..."

"What?"

"Before you hang up, remember, I called you. I need your help now, before we meet."

"Oh, yes," he replied, sounding as if he had forgotten that I was the one who phoned him. He was through talking, and he was going to hang up. "What do you need?"

"I need you to check out a corporation for me, the Committee for Honest Government. Who are on the articles of incorporation, the board of directors, that sort of thing, and run a rap sheet on each individual. Do it yourself so no one else will see the results. Bring it tonight, if you can."

"O.K.," he responded flatly. "At six."

Chapter 22

I spent the rest of the morning reviewing the other grant applications. One was a request for $12,000,000 over a three year period filed jointly by the Prisoners' Union and the American Friends Society. Carl Jenssen represented the American Friends Society, the Quakers, who have been a positive force in prison reform ever since we've had prisons. In fact, they started the Pennsylvania penitentiary system in 1829, as a humane alternative to the barbaric punishments of the day.

I'd known Jenssen, one of the leading Quaker prison reformers by reputation, and had met him once at a criminal justice educator's conference. An intense man, with a passion for fairness and humane treatment "...even unto the least of our brethren," as he put it.

Their application proposed funding six residential centers in Santa Clara County, just south of San Jose, and four spread out between Salinas and Bakersfield. Their proposal was sound in design, cost effective, and contained a good evaluation component.

The second proposal was from Delaney Road, an organization founded twenty years ago in the bay area by Marty Cohen, a moxie ex-con from New York who started with a $1,000 loan from a shylock, and rented the Turkish Embassy, abandoned at the time, located in a wealthy section of San Francisco. He filled it with parolees, and put them all to work in businesses he created all around the bay area.

To my way of thinking, the Delany Road program had consistently been the most effective approach to offender rehabilitation in the country. They had an ambitious proposal to establish twenty-four residential satellite centers in northern California the first year, each housing 200 inmates. They would establish the same rigid hierarchical structure and attack therapy method used so successfully in their main program. The second and third years, they would add twenty centers, if the population proved to be there.

The phone rang. "Hello, Dr. Worth." It was Jill.

"Matt," I interrupted.

"Not at this point in time," she replied, which meant that Ms. Reed-Wilder, the Dragon Lady, was lurking somewhere nearby. "I am just stepping out for lunch. Do you want me to get something for you?"

I looked at the clock, high noon. Where did the morning go? I knew Jill's lunch hour was just that, an hour, and it was strictly timed. "Are you sure you'll have time, Jill? I don't want to cut into your lunch."

"No trouble, Dr. Worth. Can I bring you something from Sam's Deli?"

"Sure, that sounds good. Make it a deviled egg and Swiss cheese on rye and a Royal Crown Cola, it they have it. Otherwise, make it a milk."

"I've got it. Anything else?"

"No thanks, Jill. Do you want some money now?"

"That won't be necessary. I can advance you enough until 1:00," she laughed softly, and hung up.

I began the review of four more grant proposals. None had sufficient merit to warrant further consideration. One was from a youth counselor in Yolo County whose intentions seemed good, but who offered no viable program. Another was from the Neighborhood Church of Jesus Christ and his Redeemed Followers. I've never been one to knock a person's religion or belief system, but I have always opposed any person or group who claims to have the answer, and attempts to impose it on others. This group appeared to be a cult on the fringes of fanaticism. Fortunately for me, their proposal did not meet the federal guidelines so that I could reject it without showing any overt bias.

At 1:00 p.m., or rather 12:57, Jill knocked on the edge of my open office door. I looked up startled. "One deviled egg and Swiss cheese on rye, and one RC coming up," she called out the order, and we laughed.

"Thanks, Jill, you're a doll. How much?"

"$8.26," she answered, handing me the register receipt.

"Hey, now, don't let this environment get you that well organized." We both chuckled quietly so as not to be heard. I gave her the money, right to the penny.

"Jill," I asked, trying to sound casual. "How long have you been working here?"

"About seven months. Just before Ms. Reed-Wilder was appointed."

I nearly choked on a bite of sandwich and tried to talk with my mouth full. "Seven months!" I know I showed my surprise. "I thought you were both career people with the Board when I came here. First, I learn she was recently appointed by the Governor, now you tell me that you came just before she did."

"Sorry, Matt," she interrupted, pointing at her watch and then toward the front office. I knew what she meant. "Talk to you later." She turned and left. I smiled, and for some reason I thought of Libby. *I wonder what she's doing back at my house. I should call her. I will, soon.*

Chapter 23

I arrived at the Coffee Tree Restaurant at 5:45 p.m., hoping to be early and speak to MacClanahan before Orneles arrived. As I entered the waiting area of the restaurant, I was met by a charming hostess with bright auburn hair, brown eyes, a pure white complexion, wearing a tailored olive colored pants suit, with a name tag on her lapel reading *Marci*.

"A party of one, sir?" she queried.

"No thanks, Marci. I'm meeting two men here." I was scanning the restaurant while I answered her, looking for either MacClanahan or a corner booth. I spotted them both at the same time. I knew he'd pick a corner too. He raised his hand and waved.

"There is one of them, now," I said, and pointed toward MacClanahan. She immediately led me to the booth, handed me a menu, smiled and said, "Your waitress is Sharon. She'll be with you shortly."

I shook MacClanahan's hand. "You're already on your second beer," I chided him.

"I've been here awhile, Worth. Had to have something to do to keep my arm limber." He flexed his right arm and gave me his wry smile.

"I'm glad you're here early, Mac. I didn't know soon enough to let you know in advance, but Robert Orneles, the DOJ investigator, will be joining us."

"Good. We need him. When Holden is not around, Orneles calls the shots."

"Tell me about him, Mac. Quickly if you can. He should be here any minute."

"He's top of the line. Worked ten years for Sacramento PD. Put himself through McGeorge Law School at night, but just couldn't pass the bar. Flunked six times. Must be a record. Finally, he gave up, lowered his sights a little, and joined the Justice Department as an investigator. Has been one of their best.

MacClanahan took a large swig of beer and signaled the waitress for another. She must know his signal by now. When she brought his, a Coors, I ordered a Heineken for myself. "Can Orneles be trusted in all this?" I asked.

MacClanahan grunted in a tone, as if giving me verbal criticism for the question. "Orneles helped Jessup set up this operation, enticed the Feds in by flattering Holden's ego, and promised a high profile prosecution in the end. His boss, Attorney General McNeal, is straight arrow, too. Both want to keep a lid on their investigations because neither one knew what the Governor might say. Best to keep the politicians out of harm's way. He brought in the Feds because they have the money to float our little crap game. That way McNeal doesn't tip his hand by including any of our operation in his budget."

"I thought Holden was running the show."

"That candy-ass. He couldn't run his grandmother's bobsled."

MacClanahan's description caught me by surprise, and I blurted out a laugh and spit some beer on the table. People in the booths around us stared.

"Sorry about that, Mac. Let me know when you're going to throw out another zinger, so I can be prepared."

MacClanahan smiled, and his eyes danced with childish delight at the effect of his humor. We both took long swallows of our beer. It tasted good.

"We let Holden and the Feds think they run things only because they have the money to float us and the influence to rescue us if we need it. Who knows, we might get lucky and nail these guys, whoever they are, in a big federal rap. But no way are we going to sit around waiting for that little mannequin with a temperature, Holden, tell us what to do."

I almost spit out some more beer. I was beginning to like MacClanahan more and more every minute. "Say Mac, Orneles asked to join us, and I asked him to check out some corporation records and criminal rap sheets for me. If he can come up with something, it might help clarify what we suspect."

Just then MacClanahan gave the hi-sign to someone at the restaurant entrance. It was Orneles. He was wearing a teal sweater over a white turtle-neck, dark charcoal slacks and black Italian leather loafers. I had dressed up too, with a new collared blue sweatshirt, new Levi's and blue and white Adidas. I could see him scanning me as he approached the table. His face was expressionless, but at least it lacked the arrogance that it wore when we first met in the motel.

"Mac. Dr. Worth." he greeted us, and sat down.

"Matt, please," I offered.

"O.K., Matt. I'm Bob. Now that we have our new introductions out of the way, let's get down to business."

He seemed anxious; up-tight. He handed me a folder containing several documents. Well, what do we have here?" I said, falling in with his down-to-business approach.

"I don't know about you boys," interrupted MacClanahan, "but I'm hungry." He waved over the waitress. 'We're ready to order now," he said without looking for our concurrence.

Sharon couldn't have been more than 18, dirty blond hair, pulled back into a ponytail, a flat-chested lean frame, with long full legs and hips. Probably a jogger, I thought. She had on the uniform of the day, white pinafore shell over a multi-colored blouse and white buck shoes. She was so vibrant and full of energy that she bounced rhythmically up and down just waiting to take our orders.

"I'll have that share-a-burger plate with green salad and Italian dressing," said MacClanahan, "only I'm not going to share, if you get my drift," he added, and looked at her to be certain that she understood. Then, he looked at each of us in turn. "Gentlemen, are you going to join me?"

Sharon looked at me. I hadn't even looked at the menu yet, but I said, "I'll have the same thing, only with very crisp fries and not the green salad." I figured, what the hell, I might as well add to the salt, cholesterol, and calories I had for lunch and count this as my OD day.

Orneles ordered a small Cobb salad and ice tea. MacClanahan added another Coors to his tab. I added another Heineken.

As we ate, I quietly filled them in on what I knew: Robbins, Garcia's death, and my information from Hat on Osborne and Zandi. They only nodded and grunted to indicate their understanding, as they ate, while I tried not to talk with my mouth full. The burger was a giant morsel with a the works: half-pound ground round, mustard, pickles, onions, lettuce, bacon, and cheese. It was great, but I was only half-finished when MacClanahan pushed his empty plate back and concentrated on his beer, while Orneles ordered coffee and cheese cake.

"It's not fair, guys," I said gesturing with my half eaten burger toward their empty plates. "You talk and I'll eat for a while," I mumbled to Orneles, while I jammed four fries in my mouth. I was through talking anyway.

Orneles summarized the record information he'd obtained for me. The Committee for Honest Government was a privately held corporation formed six years ago. It was actually incorporated in Nevada, of all places, undoubtedly for tax purposes, then registered here as an out-of-state corporation doing business in California. Orneles had checked with a contact of his in the Nevada State Department and learned that the articles of incorporation listed Adair Zandi as President, Mariana Teresa Natalie as vice-president, and Reza Agassi as treasurer. MacClanahan and I registered our surprise at the same time.

"Were you able to check on Agassi? I asked.

"Yes, he's a New York attorney who represents a

number of corporations, mostly Middle Eastern, and has no other regular practice. A friend of mine with the DOJ in New York says that Agassi is clean, as far as his office knows, but that several of the corporations he represents are alleged to have ties with foreign governments. He couldn't be more specific."

"What about this Mariana Natalie?" asked MacClanahan.

"Matt's information shows that she and Zandi were married, but they split the sheets in New York before he came out here."

"Then what's she doing in the corporation?"

"Interesting, huh, Mac. And more interesting is the fact that her address filed with the articles of incorporation is a P.O. Box 84697 at the main post office, right here in Sacramento."

"Does that mean that she lives here, or merely that she had an address here six years ago?" I threw it out more as a rhetorical question, than an actual one.

"I don't know," Orneles answered. "We can't check on the box number without bringing more Feds in, and we don't need their meddling just yet. We could mail something to her there using a rented box as a return address, and if it isn't returned..." He let his sentence trail off unfinished, then continued. "No! That would only make her suspicious. And we can't take the time for that anyway."

"Willie," I blurted, almost too loud.

"What?" they asked, in unison.

"Let's have your man, Willie, stake out the mail box. It's usually crowded enough in the post office, that he wouldn't look conspicuous. He could be sitting at one of the tables out of sight of the windows, filling out papers of some sort. If someone opens the box, he could tail her and report back."

"Suppose the person being tailed drives off? Does Willie have a car?" asked Orneles.

"No, but I can get him one," offered MacClanahan.

"O.K., then, have Willie meet me at..." I looked at my watch and recalled my 9:00 a.m. meeting with the Dragon Lady, "..say, 7:30 inside the main post office. I'll set him up."

We both looked back at Orneles. "What else have you got, Bob?" asked MacClanahan.

"I drew a blank on Zandi," he replied. Not even a traffic ticket. DMV shows two cars registered to him, a 2009 Jaguar sedan and a 1955 Volvo coupe."

"What does he need two cars for?" queried MacClanahan.

"Yeh," I interjected. "And what a contrast between a

new Jag and an older Volvo." I knew that the '55 Volvo was the classiest of all that line, and it was the personal car of Roger Moore in TV's *The Saint* series. I liked the style.

We all looked at each other and shrugged our shoulders. Orneles continued. "That's about it gentlemen. Let me sum up what we have: a mystery woman who might or might not be here, and who might or might not still be connected to Zandi. Zandi looks clean except that he's too clean, and has connections through the Committee with lawyer who might or might not be a involved with foreign governments, and we don't know which ones. We have one dead DEA agent, that we know of, and we are almost certain that Robbins killed him. And, we know that Robbins is dirty all the way. Maybe he acted under orders, killing Garcia, or maybe he just blew and eliminated his competition without thinking."

"Mac," I said. "You know Robbins. Tell us a little more about the kind of guy he is."

"I never did know him very well, Worth. More scuttlebutt than fact, although he was our institutional parole agent at San Quentin for a year while I was on the line."

"What sort of guy was he then?"

"Well, he was a strange sort. Seemed to have a limited understanding of people's motivations, both with staff and his parole caseload. He judged others as being either with him or against him. You were either trying to help him or get in his way. You were either going to give to him or take from him. He could get real paranoid, and several times when he got angry, he had a real temper tantrum. He always got on well with the inmates and parolees, though, because he made sure they knew he was in charge."

"Sounds like an impulsive type of guy, Mac. A guy who would see Garcia as trying to take from him, and who would just strike out to eliminate that threat, without ever considering the consequences."

"You might be right, Worth. Sounds more possible, now, when you look at it that way." MacClanahan was unconsciously nodding his head up and down and rubbing his chin. "Could be, too, that he sees you posing a similar threat."

"I know, Mac. I was thinking the same thing, as I was speaking. But if that's true, it could work to our advantage."

"How so?" asked Orneles.

"We might be able to set him up, smoke him out," I said. A plan had been formulating in my head as I listened to

MacClanahan's description of Robbins. "Suppose I confront Robbins and tell him he's out. That I know what he's up to and I want his action. Tell him I made a deal with the higher-ups to waste him and take over his deal."

"How are you going to get to him?" asked MacClanahan. "What if Monroe is with him? Monroe is not going to let you get to Robbins, no matter what."

"Wait a minute, Mac, let me finish. In fact, Monroe is part of it. See, I threaten Robbins to take him out, on the encouragement of his bosses. I let Monroe jump me, knock me out and the two of them take off. You follow them to see whoever they meet. Then, we might have them all."

"Suppose Monroe doesn't just knock you out. Suppose he takes you out in the country and cuts you open from asshole to appetite. Suppose Robbins doesn't know the top brass and goes after some middleman. Suppose..."

"O.K., Mac. O.K., so I didn't think the whole thing all the way through," I said, trying to imitate Alan Alda's expression of his line in the movie *Same Time Next Year*. "It's the beginning of a plan, anyway. Let's work on it."

Orneles sat up. He seemed excited to add something. "I think Matt might have an idea. Try this variation. Do you think you can get Robbins alone like you did in his motel?"

"Sure," I responded.

"O.K. Once the two of you are alone, you shove a gun in his face and tell him what you just said. That you made a deal with his boss and he's out. Force him to get into his car and drive you where you say. I'll have two city cops that I know, who owe me a favor pull Robbins over on a traffic offense, a few blocks down the road from his motel, at a pre-arranged spot. They think you look hinky, make you get out of the car, pat you down and find the gun. Robbins says you kidnapped him and were going to kill him. He's got a badge and they know him. They put you in the black and white, and Robbins takes off to find his boss, or whomever. We'll tail him just to learn who he meets. Then, we back off and re-group."

"What if it's like Mac says, Monroe tries to stop me?"

"Shoot the son-of-a-bitch, "Orneles said coldly. "It will only add a touch of sincerity to your intentions toward Robbins. In fact, that might be the better way to handle it. Let Monroe see you or hear you, then shoot him. Yea, that's a nice touch." Orneles was smiling, almost leering, as he spoke.
He was serious, deadly serious. No pun intended.

"I can't lure Monroe out like that and just shoot him."

"Why not?" asked MacClanahan, "He's a bad ass. He's going to get it sooner or later. Anyway, I agree with Orneles. Shooting him would sure get Robbins' attention. He'd know you meant business. Probably shit his pants on the spot. You'd have to let him go back inside and change."

Both MacClanahan and Orneles were laughing now, holding their noses and waving their hands to blow away the smell they simulated of Robbins' dirty pants. This seemed out of character for Orneles.

"Sorry, guys, " and I got very serious. "I can shoot someone to save my life or the life of someone else, but I'm not about to commit cold blooded murder for anyone or any cause."

"I know, Worth," said MacClanahan, consoling me with his tone and a pat on the arm. "We didn't mean it. We just got carried away with the idea of it all." He looked over at Orneles.

"That's right, Matt. We know you wouldn't do anything like that and we wouldn't ask you to."

I was not sure if they meant it or not. I felt as though they were patronizing me now. Maybe they got carried away, like Mac said, or maybe they showed their true colors. At least they know how I feel. "O.K. guys, forget it. I believe you didn't mean it, but I agree, it sure would give Robbins a start," and we all laughed together, and were once again united in pursuit of our common enemy.

"That sounds like a plan, Bob. Are you sure you can trust those two cops to play this straight?"

"No problem, Matt. Jim Pettigrew and Ron Swift. We used to work together when I was on the force. We've been washing each other's hands ever since. All we need to do is set up a time when they're on duty."

"Great," I said. "So we have Willie on stakeout at the post office and your two cops ready to take me out of Robbins' car. Maybe we should give Willie a few days before we shake up Robbins."

"I agree," said Orneles, looking first at me, then at MacClanahan. "Let's give him through the rest of the week. Have him check with Matt, here, Monday morning, if no one has checked the box by then. Call me Matt, and we'll set up the traffic stop. Robbins has never seen me so I'll tail him myself. It will feel good to get out in the field again."

"One question. It just occurred to me that whatever Robbins does or wherever he goes, I've tipped my hand with him and he'll be looking for me. Suppose he checks the jail and they have no record of me?"

"That's easy," responded Orneles. "I'll have Pettigrew and Swift book you on paper for kidnap and assault and have the record show that you bailed out, pending a formal complaint from the victim. That will dump the matter back on

Robbins."

"O.K. That solves part of the problem, but Robbins will still be after me, and so might others. We need to bring this entire case together quickly once we let Robbins go."

"You're right, Matt, of course," said Orneles, and I think we can. In fact, I think we can use this plan for a double scam. I'll have two of my own investigators with me in separate cars, when Robbins gets pulled over. We'll all follow his using the leap frog method. He can't lose all three of us. After he makes contact with whomever, we'll take him into protective custody, as it were. We can isolate him for as long as necessary."

"What about his rights?" I asked.

"Fuck his rights. He'll get rights when I decide to give them to him."

It bothered me hearing someone sworn to uphold the law say he was above the law, and could exercise his own discretion about someone's rights. What unchecked power we give to those who sometimes choose to abuse it for the greater good, as they say. I'm not a naive kid, but it always surprises me how easily government agents can rise above their own ideals.

These situations have come up before when I've worked with various police agencies, especially the old-school

FBI agents. In the past, I had been able to either step out of the situation or to control it to insure a legal process and outcome.

This time, however, I did not want to step out of it. We had come too far to lose the case now and I was in too deep to want out. I consoled myself with the idea that law and order often are in conflict, and that the opportunity would arise at some future point where I could put everything right, and I could rise above my own ideals as well, at least for now.

"O.K., Bob, it's your show, "I said. So what's the double scam?"

"I'm assuming that Robbins is on the bottom link of the food chain, and that he'll only contact the person on the next link above him. As soon as we can identify that person, you confront him or her with the same scenario. You're cutting yourself in and he or she is out. When we reach that point, we'll work out the details of allowing an escape and a tail to the next link in the chain. Hopefully, it will be to the top link.

"Let's take one step at a time," said MacClanahan. "I'm with you up to the point where we isolate Robbins. We can decide then what to do next. We can't see that far ahead now."

MacClanahan stated his position firmly and in a manner that refused a challenge. Orneles paused, and then nodded his agreement. I agreed completely with MacClanahan.

"Sounds good, Mac. Anything else we need to consider?" I looked at Orneles, then at MacClanahan.

"Nothing I can think of," said Orneles.

"Nothing, really," said MacClanahan, "except somewhere along the way we'll have to let the Sacramento PD in on what we know about Garcia's killing. Also, we should tell Holden or Jamison about it. He is one of theirs, you know."

"I know, Mac, " said Orneles. "Let me handle that. Right now I think we should keep everything to ourselves. I'll contact Holden when the time is right. I don't want him screwing it up now."

"You're the boss on this, Bob, "said MacClanahan. He picked up the check. "It's on me, boys."

As we rose to leave, I put $5.00 on the table between my beer glass and the plate. "For the tip."

"Speaking of Garcia," I said, as we walked toward the door. "Has anyone seen anything about it in the papers?"

They each nodded their head no. I saw a newsstand outside the front door. "I'll get a copy of today's *Bee* while you're paying the bill."

I walked outside, put 25 cents in the slot and lifted out a paper. There it was on the second page:

UNIDENTIFIED MAN FOUND HUNG IN WAREHOUSE

Police today said that an unidentified Mexican male was found dead in a warehouse at about 11:30 p.m. last night. Police responded to the scene after receiving an anonymous phone call to check the warehouse at 1153 Bryan Street in the industrial area off of East Arden Way. They found the man hanging from the rafters in the second story of the building. Police have no suspects in the case, but are hoping to identity the victim soon, from finger prints.

"Oh, oh" I said, looking up at Orneles who had been reading over by shoulder. Once the cops run those prints, they'll come back blank, but a red flag will pop up in the DEA's computer."

"I'll handle it," Orneles replied. "We set up a phony rap sheet in DOJ files on Garcia. I'll send you a copy. The police won't suspect a thing." Orneles seemed so sure of himself, so I let it go.

MacClanahan joined us and we showed him the news story. Orneles gave him the same assurances.

"Thanks, Mac. That was a great dinner. I'm stuffed. I'll have to remember this place," I said.

"Yes, thanks, Mac," Orneles joined in. "You have the slush fund to pay for benefits like this. I'll stay in touch."

We said good night and headed toward our vehicles. I had parked my pickup as far away from other vehicles as I could, being overly cautious about my own safety and the safety of others around me, since Garcia's death. I took the remote switch out of my pocket and turned it on to start my engine.

Kaboom, went the loudest explosion I had heard in years. I instinctively fell back and ducked behind the nearest car and looked. The sky was full of little pieces of my Chevrolet pickup.

"Damn." said Orneles, as he joined me behind the car.

"Christ on a crutch," hollered MacClanahan. What the hell happened?" And he joined us.

I showed them my remote switch. They understood immediately.

"You're pushing somebody's button, Matt," Orneles said.

"I guess, but who knew we were going to be here? And, how did they know?" One of us must have been followed, I thought. Or someone's office or phone is bugged.

Chapter 24

The Vacaville fire and police were there in force and had the area controlled within two minutes. Two officers were looking our way, and I knew that they would want to talk with me.

Orneles saw the officers too, and was quick to respond. "Matt, you go on into the police station with them, but don't say anything on the way. I know the chief. I'll get him on the phone and somehow and put a lid on this."

"I'll wait for you at the police station, Worth, and give you a ride home," said MacClanahan. "I need to go into Sacramento and get Willie set up with a car, and arrange for him to meet you in the morning."

My pickup had just been blown all over the parking lot and the nearby orchard, and they were talking as if it was routine. "O.K.," I said to each of them.

I walked toward my truck, still looking dumb-founded. The engine and top of the cab were gone. The left fender, frame, truck bed, and rear wheels were all that remained. Small pieces of glass and metal crunched under my feet as I walked. Any semblance of a fire had been extinguished by the quick-acting firemen. Now they were beginning to pick up the pieces.

"I'm Officer Boyd," a voice said to the right of me. "Is this your vehicle?" I turned toward the sound. A female police officer was standing four feet away. She was tall, about 5'10', 140 pounds, with straw-blond hair cut in a pageboy, high cheekbones, and a well-tanned face with full lips, with no lipstick, and deep, rich brown eyes. She saw me looking at her.

"Excuse me, sir. Is this your vehicle?" she repeated. She was direct, but friendly.

"Oh...yes...what's left of it. I never should have used that super unleaded gas," I said, trying to sound casual, when I was still in a state of awe.

"Sir, I doubt that using super unleaded gas was the cause of your problem." I sensed that she knew I was going to jest with her, flirt with her, if you will, and that she would play along to the extent that she didn't lose control of the situation.

"Yes, I think you're right, officer. Let's go down to the station where I can explain what I know."

"May I see your license, please, sir?"

"Oh, sure." I gave her my license. She copied all the data onto her report form and returned it.

"Here you are, Mr. Worth. Thank you."

She twisted the radio mike pinned to her shoulder toward her mouth and summarized to dispatch what had occurred and that we were coming into the station. Then, she waved once to another officer standing on the other side of my truck, and we got into her police cruiser.

As she was backing up to avoid running over one of my headlights lying in the road, I observed a wedding band on her finger. When she straightened out and started forward, she held up her ring finger. "Did you want to see this?" she asked.

"You don't miss much," I quipped.

"I hope not," she replied, and her lips parted into a slight smile. "Now, tell me Mr. Worth, what do you think happened to your pickup?"

"Well, I think it blew up." I tried not to sound too sarcastic.

"Yes, Mr. Worth, I'd say that is an accurate description of what occurred. Now, why or how do you think that happened?"

"It's a long story." I said. "I can explain it all when we get to the station." She gave me a long questioning look, a slight smile still evident in the corners of her mouth, as if she was humoring me.

"Hey, I'm not trying to put you on, or anything." I said.

She looked forward and didn't say another word until we were inside the station, seated in what appeared to be a squad room or briefing room. I hoped that Orneles had been able to reach the Chief.

"How about some coffee, Mr. Worth?" She was impersonal, but pleasant.

"Sure, I'll have a cup. Thanks. And, it's Matt. You can call me Matt, if you want."

"Here you are, Mr. Worth. Now, let's talk about that exploding pickup of yours."

"To be honest with you, Officer Boyd, this is one of those situations that isn't easy to explain."

"Why don't you give it a try. I've got all night to listen."

"I'm sorry, Officer Boyd, but I need to collect my thoughts. I don't know where to begin." I was trying to stall, hoping that Orneles had been able to reach the Chief, but I wasn't doing a good job of it. Officer Boyd was on the verge of losing her patience with my stalling.

Just then the door opened, and a large man filled the doorway. He was about 60, heavy set, with gray curly hair around the fringes, and balding on top. Officer Boyd stood up, almost coming to attention.

"Dr. Worth, I'm Chief Bates," he said, coming forward to shake my hand.

"Chief, it's my pleasure," and a relief, too, I thought.

"I'll take it from here, Officer Boyd," he said, giving her a commanding look.

"But, Chief, I was…."

"Officer Boyd." His voice was quiet, but stern.

"Yes sir," she said. Her face reddened, as she tried to hide the indignation in her voice. "Excuse me." And she passed between us and out the door.

"Nice meeting you, Officer Boyd," I called after her "Maybe we can talk again some time." *Why do you have to be a smart ass, I said to myself.*

"You're free to go, Dr. Worth." the Chief said. I don't know what this is all about, but Bob Orneles has assured me that he must keep us all like mushrooms for a while, 'in the dark and covered with bull shit.' He laughed at his own joke. "Anyway, I hope whatever you're doing works out."

"Thanks, Chief. We appreciate all your cooperation. I can second what Orneles said. We are into something very sensitive, and we wouldn't want it to blow up in our faces like my truck did. I'm sure Orneles will brief you when he can."

Chapter 25

I walked out the front door and found MacClanahan parked in front, waiting. We headed for Sacramento.

I asked MacClanahan to drive me to the airport rather than home, so I could rent a car. Tomorrow I would call AAA and report the loss of my truck and learn what amount the insurance would pay toward my loss. MacClanahan told me that Holden had a contingency fund in his operation and that if we leaned just right, Holden would pay the difference between what AAA paid and the cost of a new truck. I thought that was a great idea.

I rented a car at the airport, a new Buick, and drove home. Before entering my apartment, however, I wedged a pencil between the hood and body, and broke it off. Hopefully, if anyone opened the hood, the pencil would fall out unnoticed. My apartment door was unlocked. I opened the door and entered as quietly as possible. Carla was sitting on the living room couch reading my Elmore Leonard novel again. She looked up and smiled as I entered.

"Hi! I'm almost finished," she said, holding up the book to show me her place.

"You must have been reading for a long time." I looked at my watch; 10:25 p.m.

"Just about an hour. I'm a fast reader. I stopped by for a night cap. You weren't here, but I thought you would return soon, so I let myself in to wait. Besides, I had to finish this novel."

"Well put it down now so you will have a reason to come back." She had risen from the chair and started toward me slowly, as we spoke. I was moving toward her.

"I don't need to find a reason, Matt," she said in low guttural tones, trying to sound as animalistic as she could. "Not when you're here." We kissed. It was long and wet, and I let her lips envelop mine. I forgot for the moment what happened to my truck and concentrated on Carla and the loving she offered.

"What about that night cap," I asked.

"Maybe later," she replied, as she kissed me again, smiled, then walked into the bedroom, peeling off her clothes and dropping them on the floor one by one, leaving a trail for me to follow. I did. Rather, I should say that we did, because my frontal protrusion was leading the way. By the time I reached the bed, it was so ready that my shorts got caught trying to slip them off, and I almost fell off the bed. *That will teach me to hurry.*

Later, we showered, dried each other, and then lay sitting up in bed talking.

"I'll have that night cap now!" she said.

"What would you like?" I asked.

"Whatever you are going to have."

I filled two three-ounce glasses with crushed ice, then filled them with Brugal rum, adding a slice of orange for character. "Here's to you," I said, as I handed Carla her drink. We touched glasses as if toasting something that we both understood, and then took sips.

"Hum, that's good. What is it?"

"Rum," I answered, but not just any rum. That's Brugal Rum straight from the factory, located deep in the heart of the Caribbean. I waved my glass around and spoke in dramatic tones, as if offering her a soliloquy from some great play. She must have viewed it more as a comic opera, because she laughed, put two fingers in her glass, then flipped rum on my stomach.

I told Carla about my truck by saying I was having dinner with a business associate, when someone put a bomb in my truck and blew it all over the parking lot. I skipped the part about the remote starter and played down the incident as some sort of local youth gang retaliation gone awry. Someone hit the wrong truck. She merely listened, acknowledged how glad she was that I wasn't hurt, and accepted my story without question.

I thought that most women would have been more curious and had me explain everything in greater detail. I was glad she hadn't because I did not want to lie any more than I had to, and I didn't know how far to trust her with the truth. When this is all over, I thought, I am going to tell her everything, and see if we can develop one of those open and complete relationships. Something I'd experienced only once, with my wife some years ago.

Carla stayed the night, at least until 5:00 a.m., when she returned to her own apartment. I laid there thinking of Libby, and for some reason I felt guilty for being with Carla. *I miss you Libby.*

Chapter 26

The next morning, as I prepared breakfast, I put on a selection of my CDs. The first song was *Aquellos Ojos Verdes*, aka *Green eyes*. It was the old Jimmy Dorsey arrangement first recorded in 1941, with a duet by Helen O'Connell and Bob Eberly. It was my song for Libby. The refrain was *Those green eyes that I never will kiss.*

I phoned my home in Oak Grove, and it rang and rang and rang. *Come on, Libby, pick it up.* Finally a faint voice said "Hello."

"Libby, it's me, Zee. How are you doing?"

"Well, hi Zee. I couldn't imagine who would be calling so early until Perry said it might be you."

"Perry? Perry who? You remember I told you not to have any stay-overs...."

"Perry, you know. Your next door neighbor. He's been teaching me to garden, Zee. We're planting corn and string beans this morning, and we planted tomatoes yesterday. He's also been teaching me how to cook Italian style. We're having a great time. I cooked dinner for him on Monday and he cooked for me on Friday.

"Good, Libby. I'm...a...glad to hear it."

"What do you want, Zee?"

"Huh?"

"What do you want, Zee? Why did you call?"

"I.....a..... just want to see how you were doing, that's all."

"Good, Zee. I'm doing good"

"That's good, Libby. That's nice. I just thought I'd check. I have to be off to work now. I should be home for a weekend soon. Bye, Libby"

"Bye Zee."

I wanted to say more, but I couldn't think of anything appropriate to say. I'm not usually at a loss for words like this.

Chapter 27

I checked the hood of the car. The pencil was just where I had left it. I started the engine, waited a few seconds, then breathed deeply. Pretty dumb, I thought. What did I think I would do if someone had wired in a bomb and replaced the pencil? A rhetorical question, at best.

I met Willie at 7:30 a.m. at the post office. He seemed to know what to do, and had brought some forms and papers to use in pretending his presence was legitimate. We found the mail box and he found a perfect location to wait, out of view of postal clerks at the windows. I gave Willie my card and cell phone number and instructed him to call immediately if someone checked the mail box. Then, I drove to work.

As I entered the BOC door, Ms. Reed-Wilder met me at the reception counter. "Good morning, Dr. Worth. May I have the briefs you've prepared on the grant proposals so that I can study them before our 9:00 o'clock meeting?"

The words she used put her statement in question form, but her tone was a demand, or at least a firm request. I thought she was even hoping that I had not prepared any briefs so that she could play *Gotcha*.

"Yes, of course. Here you are. See you at 9:00." I was proud of myself for having anticipated her game.

"Yes, thank you." I detected a note of disappointment in her voice.

I walked into my office and was barely seated when the phone rang. "Hello. Dr. Worth here."

"Matt, it's Orneles. Can you talk?"

"Yes, of course. I can do that, but it would be better if you used this number." I gave him my cell phone number. "It's clean." I hoped he would understand my caution. He called my cell phone immediately.

"Matt, the police identified Garcia from his prints. I told you that we made up a phony record on him just in case anyone checked him out. It shows two prior petty thefts, one prior assault, and one trespass. The police also know he recently obtained a five year lease on the warehouse where he was killed. You were right about the red flag going up at DEA. Garcia's boss called Holden and he called me in a fit because we hadn't told him. He scheduled a meeting with me, MacClanahan, Jessup, and Jamison. He expects a detailed accounting of what you've done and what we know, but you're not invited. He also said he'll tell me how we will proceed with this operation."

"Does this mean that our recent discussion will become just idle talk?" I thought my phrasing was appropriate.

"Hard to tell at this point. I think I can pacify Holden and stall him on any new direction to take. Leave it to me. I just wanted you to know about the identification of Garcia. I'll call you at home tonight and fill you in on my meeting with Holden."

"I can hardly wait," I said, with a little sarcasm in my voice. The phone went dead.

I phoned Sacramento Police and asked to speak to the detective investigating the Garcia murder. I was put on hold for at least two minutes. Finally, a Sergeant Brock answered. I explained who I was and that I had heard about the murder, and that I was calling to determine if my grant applicant, Garcia, and the dead man were one in the same. He grilled me on how I had learned about the name of the murdered man because to his knowledge, Garcia's identity had not been released. I stonewalled him and said there must be a leak in his office somewhere because the media had the name. He fumed for several minutes, but finally we exchanged enough personal information about Garcia that I could confirm openly what I already knew. He said he wanted to talk to me about my knowledge of Garcia in more detail, and that he would call later for an appointment.

I looked at my watch, 8:59. Just in time. I walked up the hall to Ms. Reed-Wilder's office and knocked.

"Come in, Dr. Worth."

I glanced toward Jill before opening the door. She was talking on the phone and didn't notice me standing there.

"Sit, please, Dr. Worth." She gestured toward an arm chair positioned facing her at the side of the desk. I sat down as if on command.

"I need to make one modification in my brief before we proceed."

"Oh?" she queried.

"Yes. The applicant named Garcia is dead. We can disregard his proposal." She tried to keep her composure, but she flinched when I said dead, and began bouncing the eraser end of her pencil on the desk.

"Dead! How do you know it was him?"

That seemed like an odd way to phrase a question. Wouldn't it be more natural to ask, "Are you sure" or "How did it happen?" Maybe she already knew he was dead and was merely surprised that I knew.

"How do I know it was him?" I asked.

"Garcia. How do you know he is dead?"

Now I wasn't sure how to interpret her reaction. I better just move on. "Do you remember reading in yesterday's paper about a man found hanged in a warehouse?"

"Yes. What a horrible thing."

"It was him." I left it at that hoping to bait her.

"But the news article called him an unidentified man." She let her voice hang in the air with the question implied. Her expression was intense.

"I know, but I heard on the radio news this morning that he had been identified through his prints. The reporter gave his name and description. It sounded like the same Garcia, so I phoned Sergeant Brock at the PD to confirm it. It was."

"I heard two newscasts on KPQL this morning, and nothing was said on either one about Garcia. What station were you listening to?"

"I really don't know. I'm not familiar with the radio stations in this area yet. I just turned the dial until I found one that sounded clear."

We reviewed the applications and she seemed impressed with Robbins. In fact, she insisted that I personally visit his proposed sites in the lower valley towns. She even suggested that Robbins might be able to take over the warehouse leased by Garcia, and expand his program. She was totally insensitive to Garcia's death. It was a short visit, and I left with my marching orders.

Chapter 28

I returned to my office, packed my briefcase with the files on Robbins' proposal sites, and checked out with Jill. I told her I was going out in the field. I didn't tell her where because I didn't want anyone to know where to find me. Before unlocking my car, I checked for the pencil jammed under the hood. No problems indicated. I was going to have to buy some more pencils.

I took old Highway 99 south to Stockton, and then on to Tracy, and finally cut east over to Modesto, where I made a visual inspection of the sites proposed by Robbins. All three were basically the same: small abandoned shopping centers, with an abandoned motel, located on the fringes of decaying neighborhoods. They all showed the same potential, that with a little elbow grease and handyman repairs, they would fit what Robbins wanted, inexpensive property that could accommodate 200 to 300 parolees. For the first time, my investigation really was cursory. In Modesto, I didn't even get out of my car. And, I was not about to drive to Fresno at this point. By noon, I was beginning to feel feverish and achy, as though I was coming down with the flu.

By 4:00 p.m., I was approaching Bakersfield, and really feeling lousy, with cold chills, even in this 96 degree heat. I thought a beer might revive me, so I pulled off the freeway and drove into what looked like a combination truck stop and road house named 'The Saddle Bags'. *One drink and then I better find a motel for the night, I thought.*

Rows of truck and trailer outfits and 40 foot vans with sleeper tractors filled the huge asphalt parking area to the rear, where the fuel pumps were located. They probably had showers and cots there, too. As I got out of my car, the din of twenty to thirty Cummins diesel engines idling filled the air. They make a nice sound.

When I entered the bar area, I felt the temperature drop at least 20 degrees. The large room was laid out like an old western bar, with a long mahogany bar top, round bar stools, and a brass foot rail. A long mirror behind the bar reflected a vast array of liquor bottles and cowboy memorabilia. Paintings of western scenes hung on the walls around the room.

There was an elevated stage at the end of the bar area, with room for a small band, and a 12 by 20 foot hardwood floor area in front for dancing. The sign above the stage said, *Bobby Clyde Puckett and the Purple Sage Boys, live every Friday and Saturday nights.* The rest of the cafe was about 40 by 20 feet, filled with large round oak tables, each holding four to six chairs. The kitchen and bathrooms were off the end of the bar to the rear.

The tables were filled with a mixture of truck drivers, construction workers and local cowboy types, having beer, sandwiches, chips, pretzels, peanuts, and jerky. Everyone seemed to be having a good time, and the noise from the conversation and laughter was high-pitched and constant. It almost matched the din of the diesel engines outside.

I sat on a stool at the end of the bar, put my shoes on the rail, and ordered a Bud draft. It came in a frosty glass, with a two-inch head, and it was cold. I drank half the glass just to quench my thirst, then sipped the other half between handfuls of peanuts from a bowl placed in front of me by the bartender.

In my spare time at home, when I had any, I played on an old Martin guitar and sang old country songs from the '40s. I had always told my friends that in the next life I want to be a lead guitar player in a honky-tonk bar in Bakersfield. Now I wasn't sure.

Several patrons at the bar were shaking poker dice or liars dice with each other or the bartender, a tall heavy set man with brown curly hair and a handlebar mustache, wearing Wrangler jeans and a cowboy shirt. Jake was his name, and he pounded the bar with the dice cup and bellowed out a roar of laughter each time he won, which seemed to be often. He looked like a whiskered Lon Chaney.

A chunky blond in her mid-40's named Pattie worked behind the bar with Jake. She also wore Wranglers and a cowgirl-styled blouse with the top two snaps undone in an undisguised effort to feature the fullness of herself, barely contained in her up-lift bra. She reminded me of Dolly Parton. She was all smiles and honeydew, as well.

She walked over to the juke box and inserted two coins. Patsy Montana's voice and yodeling filled the room for five minutes. Bob Wills and his Texas Playboys followed with their classic rendition of *San Antonio Rose.*

Suddenly, I had the feeling that a man sitting near the other end of the bar was staring at me and, perhaps, trying to get my attention. I could just barely see him out of the corner of my eye, and I did not look directly at him because I did not feel like having company. I ordered a second draft and shot a quick glance in his direction, as the bartender walked away from me. I was hoping that his gaze would follow her. Instead, he left his stool, walked to my end of the bar and sat on the stool next to me.

"Dr. Worth, isn't it?" He said it more as a statement than a question. I could not imagine who would recognize me or know me in this part of the country, and especially in this bar. I turned toward him, stared blankly for a few seconds, and then suddenly recognized him as Fred Willows, one of the corrections training consultants who worked out of the BOC. I had only seen him twice in the office since that first morning at coffee. He must be out in the field most of the time.

"Fred!" I exclaimed. "You took me by surprise. The last thing in the world I expected was to meet someone here I knew. What on earth brings you to this neck of the woods?"

"Well, you probably don't know that Kern County is part of my beat, as I call it. I've been here a week, now, working with the local probation department in developing a variety of in-service training programs that meet BOC requirements."

"Sounds like nice duty, Fred. Come here often, do you?" I said that in jest, but it came out sounding serious and he took it that way.

"Actually, I do, Dr. Worth. The food is great, and I can get lost in the crowd. Also, it provides a fascinating study in human behavior, if you're into that sort of thing."

"Yea, I'll bet. This place must really shake and rock on Friday and Saturday nights when Bobby Clyde and his boys get to thumping their guitars and twanging out *Love Sick Blues*."

We both laughed at the image that emerged, but it was a fond laughter on both our parts. I liked old fashioned country music, and thought that it well reflected both the rich and the haunting experiences and feelings of a sub-culture whose members lived life directly, without pretenses or masquerades.

Fred was scanning the crowd by looking in the mirror over the bar He was either a voyeur, a student of human nature, or just plain horney. He was about 51, medium build, with thick reddish-blond hair that was parted in the middle and combed straight back in a way that made his face appear oval. He wore brown cords, desert boots, and a yellow herringbone slip-over shirt.

"Tell me, Fred, how long have you been at BOC?"

"Twenty-one years, now. I came aboard shortly after the Standards and Training for Corrections Program (STP) was created by the Legislature."

"How has it been, working for Ms. Reed-Wilder?"

"Not too bad, really. I am out in the field much of the time, and she lets me do my own thing. When I'm in the office, she's a little too tight, too controlling, but then I figure she's new and needs to get comfortable supervising us old hats, before she can relax."

"Stapleton was the director before, right?"

"Yes, and he was a great guy, too, and really supportive of our program efforts. The morale was better when he was here.

"Do you know why he was fired?"

"No, Dr. Worth. Two days after Governor Osborne took office, Stapleton called us all together in the office and explained how political his job was, and that he was being replaced by a new appointee. He was gone the next day and Ms. Reed-Wilder was in. I think we were all in shock for a week or so, but we're used to her now. Actually, she has been a real advantage for us in one way, because of the political influence she seems to have."

"How so?"

"Well, it's almost as if she's in the sack with the Governor. Anything we need, she gets. Our budget and salaries will increase 10% effective July 1, and for once we are holding positive thoughts for the future."

"In the sack! That certainly is a descriptive phrase, Fred. Do you mean that she and Osborne are actually sleeping together?"

"Oh, no, Dr. Worth. I meant it figuratively, not literally.

I'm sure they're not actually boinking, it's just that she has such direct access to him and influence over him, that they do seem close."

"I get the picture, Fred. I appreciate you sharing your observations with me. It's amazing what a difference one person can make in the use of taxpayer's money. He gave me a questioning look, trying to figure out exactly what I meant by my comment. I wouldn't tell him how satisfied I was to hear that their relationship was close.

Someone had put some coins in the juke box, and the gravelly voice of T. Texas Tyler came blaring out with the song *Remember Me*; one of my all-time favorites. I looked at my watch, 5:38 p.m., and now I felt sleepy as well as lousy.

"I have to go, Fred. Nice talking to you." I rose from my stool and patted him on the back and headed out the door.

"You too, Dr. Worth. See you in church."

I headed for the motel strip, checked in at the Western Roundup Inn, and crashed on the bed. It was late morning when I awoke. I was still feeling feverish.

Chapter 29

It was nearly 3:45 p.m. the next day when I arrived back in Sacramento, so I drove directly to my apartment. It was still 88 degrees outside, but I was shivering with cold. I opened my apartment door and entered, not caring whether anyone was inside. I threw my coat and tie on the chair, went into the kitchen and poured a large *Jose Cuervo* over ice. It tasted good, but made me shiver more.

I took the *Cuervo* into the bedroom, set it on the nightstand, went into the bathroom and washed down three aspirin with an AIka-Seltzer, stripped naked and got into bed. I felt sure that I drifted in and out of sleep, and I had vague recollections of aching and shivering and flashing from hot to cold. At one point I had this weird dream that I was lying naked on top of the bed and a woman was pouring cold liquid all over my body and rubbing it in.

Eventually, I stirred and became aware of sounds and smells. I was waking up and I felt much better. I rose up on one elbow, and looked out into the living room. Daylight was streaming through the curtains so I assumed it was morning. The fever broke and the flu must have left during the night, like I thought it would. The smell of fresh coffee drifted in from the kitchen, and then I heard someone pouring a cup.

"Who's out there?" I called.

Carla appeared in the doorway, wearing light blue denim shorts and a print blouse, with the shirttail tied in a knot in front. "Hey, sleepy head. I didn't think you were ever going to wake up. How do you feel?"

"Fine, I think. I can tell better after I get up and walk around."

"Want some coffee?"

"Love some." She left and returned with two cups, handed me one, and sat on the edge of the bed drinking hers.

"I stopped by Friday after I tried calling you at work, and the receptionist said you hadn't come into work and they hadn't heard from you."

"Friday," I blurted. "What day is today?"

"Sunday, and its 4:14 p.m."

I was stunned. I had slept two days. Carla explained that my fever had remained high until last night, when it broke. She had stayed with me the entire time, sleeping on the couch a few hours at a time, and giving me alcohol rubs when I became delirious with fever. I expressed by gratitude and my embarrassment over causing her such inconvenience.

"I was afraid the fever would burn you up and render you impotent," she said, laughing. "If that happened, I was going to let you croak."

"You're a sweetheart," I said, warmly, squeezing her leg with my hand.

"Why don't you shower while I cook us something to eat," she said, and she rose from the bed and walked into the kitchen.

The shower felt great, and I let the hot beads of water beat down across my back, shoulders, and the back of my neck for several minutes before and after I washed. Finally, I turned off the water, dried, slipped on a pair of shorts, and went out into the kitchen to help Carla. She was cooking omelets, with cheese, black olives and sausage. She also had diced potatoes and fried them, and prepared a hollandaise sauce on the side. She had even made a blender of Brugal rum fizzes. When everything was ready, we took the food on trays, out by the pool area to eat. I was hungry.

"Delicious," I said between bites.

"Thanks. See, you're not the only one who can cook."

"You can cook for me anytime," I replied, and I looked at her and wondered where our relationship was going, or would go, after my job here was finished. Then I thought of Libby, and wondered what she was doing. *Was it her turn to cook for Perry...and where or when did she learn to cook? She rarely cooked anything when we were together. Of course, I was never*…I stopped my useless reverie and returned to matters at hand.

Carla and I spent the evening on the couch quietly watching TV, with neither of us saying much. Occasionally, she would reach over and scratch my back or run her fingers threw my hair, and we'd look at each other and smile. My thoughts continued off and on to drift back to Libby, and I wondered what she was doing.

Chapter 30

I arrived at the BOC in my best dark brown Dockers 3-piece suit just before 8:00 a.m. Jill was already seated at the reception desk.

"Good morning, Dr. Worth." She glanced quickly at the door of Ms. Reed-Wilder's office, cupped her hands around her mouth, winked at me and whispered, "I mean Matt."

I winked back, understanding that she meant the Dragon Lady was on duty.

"Yes, good morning Jill." As I walked by the reception counter, we each held out a hand to let them touch to express our mutual need for more intimacy than was available in the usual greeting ritual. I don't know why she had taken to me so openly, but I know that I found her to be warm and caring, and the only breath of humanness in this bureaucratic vacuum.

"Will you have lunch with me?" I whispered.

"Yes," she whispered in return. "I'd love to, but we'll need to leave right at 12:00."

"I'll be ready" I turned and started to walk toward my office, then turned back.

"Oh, by the way. I was gone Thursday and Friday to Stockton, Tracy, Modesto, and Bakersfield. Any phone messages for me?"

"No, not a one."

I went to my office, took off my coat, loosened my tie, and spent the morning preparing my investigative report on the complete proposal by Robbins. Apparently, I lost track of time, because I was startled by the buzz on my phone. I checked my watch, 11:55 a.m.

"Yes?" I knew it had to be Jill.

"Matt, this is Jill. I'm almost ready. Begin the countdown."

"I'll be right out. I checked my wallet to be sure I had enough cash of pay for lunch, and then met Jill at the reception counter. We walked out the door at high noon.

"I know a nice restaurant, Matt. We can take my car, if you don't mind."

"No, not at all." Her car was parked across the street in the state garage, stall number 74, second floor. It was a new Mercedes 190, the only model in the Mercedes line that I thought was ugly, but I wouldn't tell her that.

We parked at a garage in the center of town and walked two blocks to the Capitol Inn, an elegant restaurant where Jill assured me politicians never dined. We were seated at a window table looking out on a waterfall and pond that graced the patio area.

We ordered two dry martinis, straight up. They arrived in classic Waterford crystal glasses. We clinked them together gingerly, toasting our lunch, and took large sips.

"That tastes great," I said.

"Yes, it does. But a sinful idea," she said sarcastically. "I want you to know that I rarely take a drink during the day, and never during working hours."

"That's nice to hear. I was afraid I was dining with a lush." We laughed.

The waiter returned and we ordered lunch, a Crab Louie each. The waiter assured us that the crab was fresh and that he'd bring me extra Louie dressing.

"Tell me, Jill. The other day you said you had only worked here about seven months, just before Dragon Lady came."

"Why yes, Matt, that's right." She didn't elaborate. She had thrown the ball back into my court without leaving me an opening.

"Have you been in California long?"

"Only about eight months, actually. Before my husband died we were living in Phoenix, Arizona, where he was stationed. After his death I tried to stay on and maintain the house, but the memories were too much. I sold it and moved to California, just before Thanksgiving. It was lonely, at first, but this job came open shortly after I arrived. I don't have any special job skills, so this was perfect. I was interviewed for it on a Friday and was hired by the following Wednesday. And, here I am." She opened up her arms as if presenting herself.

"Who interviewed you?" I asked.

"What? What do you mean who interviewed me?"

"You said you were interviewed for the job on a Friday. If Ms. Reed-Wilder wasn't here yet, who interviewed you for the job?"

"The former BOC director, Ronald Stapleton, I think was his name. Why, Matt? Why are you asking that?"

The Louies arrived, and the crab was fresh, and the Louie dressing was fantastic. I was trying to make my questions flow like casual conversation, but I must have come across like an interrogator after information from a spy, because she withdrew from her usual open demeanor.

"No particular reason, Jill. I am just trying to get a better sense of the organization. I wonder how it was before DL (which meant before the Dragon Lady came)."

"I can't help you there, Matt. I can say that Mr. Stapleton was a gregarious, outspoken, and friendly man, just the opposite of DL. I was looking forward to working for him, when he told us he had been fired by the new Governor. He also told me not to worry about my position because I had civil service protection, whereas he did not," She quickly regained her composure and the warmth returned to her voice and expression.

"Who did you replace? What happened to her?"

"Gee, I don't know, Matt. I think Mr. Stapleton said she was pregnant and was quitting."

"Has Ms. Reed-Wilder ever commented on your work, or shown any resentment about you being hired by Stapleton just before he was forced out?"

"No. She's always been cordial, which is good for her. No sign of resentment."

She put her fork down and gave me a sort of knowing look. "Come on Matt. This is more than idle curiosity, or wanting to get to know about the organization. Are you trying to tell me something?"

"No, really, Jill. I was just making lunch conversation as much as anything. I don't mean to pry."

"Oh, I don't mind you prying," she said, with some enthusiasm, "I'm just wondering what you are after."

I wanted to tell her, but I knew I couldn't even give her a hint. Too much was riding on secrecy, and the way things were going, I didn't know who to trust. I had to think of something to either neutralize or divert her suspicion.

I looked her right in the eye and said, "If you want to know the truth of the matter, Jill, I'm trying to learn more about you. I like you. I think I was actually hitting on you."

I don't know what made me say it, but now that I had, I would have to run with it. Hopefully, I would be able to talk myself out of any sort of intimate relationship, if she took it that way.

She had a mouth full of salad when I spoke, and she swallowed it in one gulp. A faint blush filled her cheeks and she put one hand on top of mine. "That's sweet, Matt, but there is nothing here for you. I can't settle for being two ships that pass in the night, and I don't see the opportunity for us to be more than that." A single tear ran down her right cheek. She caught it and feigned a cough.

"We can always be friends," I said.

"I hope so. You're a nice person." Just then she looked at her watch. "Oh, oh, my time is running out. We need to start back."

It was 12:50. I left a tip and grabbed the waiter on our way toward the cashier and got the bill. She ran three yellow lights on the way back to the office. We reached the parking garage with three minutes to spare. I started to open the door, but she said, "Matt." She took my left hand in hers and kissed it gently. "I mean it. You're a nice guy. And we're going to be just friends."

At that moment, I thought of Libby. I felt a sense of relief at Jill's response, because I hadn't meant for anything more intimate to develop, and I was glad she defined the situation as she did.

Chapter 31

I returned to my office to shuffle more papers. At about 2:00 p.m. the intercom buzzed.

"Yes, Jill?"

"You have a call on line 1. A strange sounding man. He wouldn't give me his name."

"Thanks, Jill."

I picked up the phone and pushed the line 1 button. "Hello, Dr. Worth here."

"Dr. Worth." The voice was muffled. "This is Willie. You know. Mr. Mac's Willie."

"Willie, you were supposed to call me on my cell phone."

"I know, but I lost the card with the number on it, so I'm calling you there."

"Willie, let me give you my cell number."

"No, Dr. Worth. No time." Willie responded in a hushed tone. "Meet me, Dr. Worth. I can't say anything over the phone."

"Where?"

"Go to 14th and Broadway. Sammy's Cafe, on the southwest corner. I'll be inside."

"Now?"

"Sure, now. Don't you wanna know what I got?"

"Of course, Willie. I'll be there in ten minutes."

I grabbed my coat and headed for the door. "Jill, something has come up." Then I whispered, "Is You-Know-Who back from lunch yet?" and I pointed toward her door.

"No. She's still out."

"Good. When the Dragon Lady comes in tell her I'm out in the field and you're not sure when I'll be back."

I dashed out the door to my rented car. No time for jammed pencils. It started and there was no *boom*. I breathed deeply.

I found Willie seated at a corner booth in Sammy's, an old, but clean cafe located in the predominantly Black section of town. Like most capitols, Sacramento was racially segregated, primarily by economics. Willie gave me the hi-sign as I entered. Three other patrons were sitting at the counter and they followed me with their eyes as I walked to the corner booth.

"Sit down, man. You get here quick."

"Hi, Willie," we slapped palms. "What do you have? Did someone check the mail box?"

"Yeh, man. This broad, a white woman, all dressed up, comes in the post office. She walks slowly toward the boxes, you know, looking all around. Me, I was filling out a job application at the table only about ten feet away. She looks right through me, man. Don't even pay me no mind. She opens the box, takes out two envelopes and leaves." He paused to drink some beer from his glass.

"Did you follow her?" I was getting excited. Our plan had worked, and so quickly too.

"I started to follow her, man, but..."

"What do you mean, you *started* to follow her?"

"Well, I started following her, but I lost her."

Damn. I was upset, but I knew Willie had tried, and I didn't want him to feel I was blaming him. "It's O.K., Willie. Tell me about it."

She goes out of the post office, jumps in a grey convertible, and takes off down Capitol Avenue. I'm right behind her 'till we gets to Perkins. You know Perkins? It's about ten miles out Capitol Avenue, the old highway that becomes Folsom Boulevard. You know, you pass it on the way to Robbins' motel."

"You mean she went to Robbins' place?"

"I don't know, man. I'm three cars behind her when we gets to Perkins. Used to be a town. Now it's just a store and an intersection. The light turns yellow before she gets there, but she runs through it and catches the red. I'm trying to decide what to do when I sees two cop cars parked at the intersection. One takes off after her. Man, I can't get stopped by no cop, so I gots to stop at the light. She just drives on, not even stopping, and that cop, he's chasing right behind her. I kept driving after the light changed, but I never seen neither her nor the cop anywhere. That's when I calls you."

"You did fine, Willie. Did you drive out as far as Robbins' motel?"

"No, man, I don't want to risk Robbins seeing me. He thinks I'm at my sister's house all week taking care of her baby."

The waiter brought Willie another beer. I ordered one too. He brought it back right away. It was cold and tasted good, especially in this afternoon heat. Willie was looking at me with an odd expression. I couldn't tell if he was smiling or grimacing. His face was ready to burst.

"Anything else, Willie?"

"Sorry I lost her, man."

"Its O.K., Willie. We'll try it again."

"We might not needs to." His expression turned into a big toothy grin and in his hand he held a small film type 35-mm camera. He looked down at it, then back at me. I caught on.

"Willie, you mean you took her picture?"

"I sure did, man. Right over the brim of my hat when she looks through me. She don't see nothing. Got a picture of her car, too, with the license plate."

"Willie, you devil. I love you. Let me have the film." He rewound the film, removed it from the camera, and handed it to me.

"You tell Mr. Mac that I done good, Dr. Worth?"

"Willie, I'll tell Mr. Mac you done just great." He was pleased. He sat back in the booth and drank his beer. What a neat guy to have on your side. Thinking all the time, loyal, and satisfied by gratitude. A rare find. I thanked him again, paid the tab, and left enough extra to include another beer for Willie, and then drove to the nearest photo lab.

Chapter 32

I located a one-hour photo lab in a small shopping center about eight blocks west on Broadway. I told the clerk to develop and print all in 5 x 7's. She said about forty minutes. I paced back and forth near the counter for a few minutes, thinking it might encourage her to hurry. It didn't. She only had one speed, slow; but she was methodical and appeared to know what she was doing.

I finally busied myself looking through old photo magazines from a stack at the end of the counter and watched her out of the corner of my eye. She was about 16, wearing jeans, no bra, and a Doors tee-shirt. Her mousy brown hair flew in all directions as she worked. Finally, she was finished.

"Only had two exposed frames on the whole roll," she said.

"Did they print well?"

"A little blurred, but not too bad. All depends on what you want to use it for."

I breathed a deep sigh of relief. I had imagined all sorts of bad results, while hoping for at least a recognizable print.

"That's $5.95, including tax." She held out her left hand for the money while she held the photos in her right hand behind the counter. It must say something about the type of clientele she usually gets.

I paid, walked out to my car, got in, and immediately opened the envelope. I slowly took out the photos. I teased myself, raising my anticipation level to its highest. I finally removed the 5 x 7s and stared at them in disbelief. "Well I'll be go to hell," I said out loud. It was the Dragon Lady.

I flashed on the monogrammed handkerchief that she had dropped during our meeting, with the initials *MNZ* on it. I didn't give it any thought at the time, but now I understood. The initials stood for Mariana Natalie Zandi. Bingo! We'd hit it big. But what? What did we have now? Time to sit back, lay all the pieces out before me and see what fits into place.

It was early, but I drove to my apartment instead of back to the office. I couldn't face Ms. Reed-Wilder Zandi, or whatever her name was, until I determined how to respond.

I took a quick shower, slipped on a pair of shorts, and poured a *Cuervo*, and looked at her picture again.

O.K., who do we have: Zandi, Osborne, Robbins, Natalie. ZORN.

That is too easy. There must be more to it. Of course we also have Orneles, MacClanahan, Jessup and McNeal, the Attorney General. I better include Jill McCloud, too, just in case she is a plant like Natalie. And, Carla Renati, I can't forget her. Maybe Renati is an alias, too.

I better see if Orneles can check her out. He should be able to run Jill at the same time, although I couldn't believe that Jill ever had even a parking ticket. Then a thought occurred to me. I had been letting Orneles handle a number of situations, and so far, had taken his role for granted. Maybe Governor Osborne is not involved at all, and Orneles is the big "O". Who better to have on the inside?

I decided to check Jill and Carla out myself. Jill should be easy. I had a friend on the Phoenix PD. We had worked together in 2002 on an inter-state car theft ring, and had been in contact off and on until I left Nevada PD. I picked up the phone and called Phoenix information, then the Phoenix PD.

"Phoenix Police. May I help you?"

"Yes, I'm calling long distance for Sergeant. Andrew McCullum."

"You mean Capt. McCullum?"

"A...yes, Ma'am"

"May I tell him who's calling?"

"Yes. Tell him it's Matt Worth, a voice from out of his past." She put me on hold, but I waited less than a minute.

"Matt," came a voice on the other end of the phone. "You son-of-a-bisket. Who said you died?"

"Hey, Andy. Captain, is it? You must be the fair-haired boy around there."

"You know better than that, Matt. It's because I'm brilliant, handsome, and dedicated."

"Sure, Andy, and don't forget modest."

"It's great to hear from you, Matt. What have you been up to all these years?"

I gave him a five minute summary of my life since leaving Nevada, including a press release version of my present job, and led up to why I called him. "I need a favor, Andy."

"Sure, buddy. If it's legal, you got it."

"I'm doing a background on a person whose prior address was in Phoenix for many years. I don't have the exact address. In fact, all I have is a name, but if what she says is true, it should be easy to verify her residence there."

"What's the name?"

"McCloud. Jill McCloud, age about 42 to 45. Husband named William, a career air force officer, now deceased."

"How soon do you need this, buddy?"

"Yesterday."

"I'll get back to you within two hours, buddy. What's your number?"

I gave him my cell number, and then asked him a few personal questions. He filled me in on his life: two promotions, two wives, three children, golf, and a speed boat.

I decided to phone MacClanahan and tell him the news about the Dragon Lady, while I waited for Andy to call me back. I dialed his office number.

"MacClanahan," he growled.

"Mac, it's Worth".

"Worth. I thought you'd be calling me today."

"You must have spoken to Willie."

"Yea. He told me about how he'd photographed the woman. Hell, I didn't think he even knew which end of a camera to point."

"He might seem slow, Mac, but he's no dummy."

"No. He's not. He's been one of the best employees, shall we say, that I've had. Did the photo help?"

"We hit it big, Mac. Mariana Natalie Zandi is none other than our own dear sweet Ms. Reed-Wilder."

There was dead silence on the other end of the phone. I couldn't even hear Mac breathing. Finally, "Well I'll be a Highland son-of-a-bitch. Big it is, Worth. This is breaking better than I thought it could. How do you want to play it now?"

"Let's go ahead with our move on Robbins," I said. "I'll call Orneles and set it up, only I want one change. When he tails Robbins after the police take me out of the car, if Robbins goes toward BOC, Orneles can take him out of circulation. I don't think it would serve any purpose for those two to meet now. If Robbins goes in another direction, Orneles can follow. Maybe Robbins will lead us to the others." I didn't tell MacClanahan what others I suspected.

"Sounds good to me, Worth, but check with Orneles about his two buddies at Sacramento PD, Pettigrew and Swift. We need to coordinate this carefully. Get back to me soon."

I poured myself a short *Cuervo* over ice and stretched out on the couch to think. I must have fallen asleep, because right in the middle of this fantastic dream, the phone rang. The noise drew me further and further out of the dream while I fought desperately to hang in there and finish it. Finally, I jerked awake and grabbed the phone.

"Hello."

"Matt, this is Andy." I looked at my watch, three hours had passed. "Sorry to take so long, but I got involved in a heated briefing."

"No problem, Andy. Find anything?"

"Not a trace. No criminal record, no driver's license or car registration, and no credit. I checked the phone records for the past ten years. Only three McClouds. I phoned all three and they never heard of your gal. I even checked with my local air force contact. No record of a William McCloud. I think you've been stiffed, Matt."

"Looks like it, Andy." I really hadn't expected this. I was just checking her out to confirm my own beliefs about how pure she was. If anyone was real in this charade, I thought it would be Jill. "Thanks, Andy. I really appreciate it."

"Sure, buddy, anytime. Keep in touch this time."

"Right. You too."

We hung up, and I sat down on the couch and stared at a painting of a bull fighter on the opposite wall. Jill, damn you. I just couldn't believe she was in on this in any way. There must be another explanation. I couldn't deal with it any more, not now.

I phoned Orneles at his cell number and explained about the photo of Mariana Natalie Zandi and the plan for Robbins tomorrow. He said he would have to check with his two cop friends first to be certain their schedules would fit in with my time line. He returned my call within twenty minutes and said we'd have to put the deal over until Monday. Pettigrew and Swift were in Los Angeles to pick up a prisoner, and wouldn't be back on regular assignment until then. He had set the plan to begin at 9:00 a.m. on Monday.

He explained that after I kidnapped Robbins, I was to drive toward Sacramento on the old highway, now Folsom Boulevard, to Power Inn Road, and then turn left. The two

Sacramento PD officers would stop the car within the next 500 yards, arrest me, and let Robbins go. Orneles and two of his best men would follow Robbins, and either take him into protective custody or tail him to his destination, depending upon which direction he took.

It all sounded so easy. I only hoped that Robbins would cooperate, and that Orneles was straight with me. When I told him about the photo of the Dragon Lady, he registered no emotion. His only response was, "Good work." Maybe he wasn't surprised. I guess we'll find out Monday if Orneles is on the level, or if I'm dead. I did not like the latter alternative.

I arrived at the BOC office by 7:45 a.m. to avoid meeting Jill. I knew I'd have to sooner or later, but I thought that later was best. Two jail inspectors were sitting in the coffee room as I walked by the door.

"Morning, " I offered.

"Morning," they replied.

I phoned Robbins at his motel and told him that we needed to meet Monday morning to modify the evaluation component included in his proposal. I told him I had a sure-fire way to make it appealing to the Feds without really revealing the success or failure of his program. He willingly agreed to meet me at 9:00. So far, so good. I spent the rest of the day reviewing files and making some clean-up calls.

Chapter 33

Monday seemed so far off, and it left me with Friday and the weekend to prepare and/or worry. I decided that a short visit home might be in order, and a visit to Hat in Inverness sounded inviting as well. I called my home number but got the answering machine, so I left a message for Libby, saying that I would be home about 3:00 o'clock.

I drove into my driveway at my home in Oak Grove at 3:15, just in time to see Libby and Perry Schaller coming out of Perry's front door, carrying several pans covered with foil, and running over to my house. "What goes?" I asked.

Libby beamed with delight about something, gave me a quick kiss on the mouth and said, "Open the door, would you, Zee. Look," as she momentarily lifted the lid off of one pot. "We've cooked dinner."

Perry was beaming too. "Libby and I have prepared an Italian dinner fit for a king. I know it's early, Zee, but we need to eat while it's hot and fresh."

"Perry," I replied," but you're not Italian."

"I know Zee, but I love Italian cooking, and Libby has been a great helper and student. I'll make a chef out of her if you give me time."

We dined on breaded and pan-fried eggplant, fettuccini *Alfredo*, and large succulent homemade meatballs, washed down with the finest *Chianti Classico* I have ever tasted.

"Delicious! Absolutely delicious!" I said to both Libby and Perry.

"It's basic, but it's tasty and it's a good start for our cooking experiments," replied Perry.

"Experiments, Perry? What do you mean experiments?" I asked.

Libby responded, "Perry and I have been taking cooking lessons, Zee, at the college culinary school in Santa Rosa. We've had five lessons in Italian cooking, and tomorrow we begin a five lesson course in French cooking. Isn't it exciting Zee?"

She was a different Libby than I last remembered. Gone were the pretensions and flirtations that she used when she wanted something. She seemed to be honestly enthused and was raving about something outside of herself. I was reminded of how she was when we were first married and began working on refurbishing our first home together. She was such a complete woman, and a delight to be with. "It sounds great, Libby. You and Perry seem to have really hit it off."

"Matt, Libby has been wonderful," Perry interjected. "She has brought the freshness of youth into this old life, and we've enjoyed each other's company immensely. I'm hoping your job in Sacramento will last a long time. I don't want to think about spending another day without sharing a part of my life with her."

"Wow, Perry. If Libby and I were still married, I'd be getting jealous about now." I teased him as I poked him in the ribs.

"Honestly, Matt, I've been very lonesome since Florence died three years ago. I didn't know just how lonesome until Libby here offered her friendship. "

Libby placed her hand over Perry's hand and smiled warmly. "You've been a true friend too, Perry, just when I needed one."

I didn't know where this mutual admiration society was going, nor did I know just how to respond, knowing that Libby would be gone as soon as I returned from Sacramento. "So tell me more about your cooking classes," I addressed to both of them.

They shared their Italian cooking experiences at the culinary school, and the fun they had making the dinners together, and they described the French cooking classes that they were to start tomorrow. The way Perry talked, I got the impression that he was sharing a part of life with the daughter he never had. I was pleased for them both, and I was feeling a cautious curiosity about how Libby had changed, or blossomed, into the warm and caring person who was emerging; the woman I once loved.

It worked out well that I planned to spend the day with Hat in Inverness, since they were going to spend the entire day at the culinary school. I phoned Hat and arranged a short sail around Tomales Bay and a picnic lunch on Hogs Island. Hat was sarcastic about how I finally condescended to spend a day out of my busy schedule with him, but I knew he was pleased.

That night, as I lay in bed, I could hear the sounds of crickets in the yard outside, and of a few neighbor dogs barking at the shadows. I thought I could hear Libby turning restlessly in her bed. I could feel the heat of my body and the yearning that rumbled inside, and for a moment I wished that Libby would come into my bed, naked, and we would make love, *just for old time sake.* But I knew that the old times were gone.

What will the new times bring, Zee, old boy? What's happening now, here with Libby?

Chapter 34

When I arrived at Inverness, I went first to Tod Lassen's boathouse, on the edge of town, where I kept my *Point Jude Daysailer*. My boat was nothing fancy, but it was fast, and easy to sail right up to a beach. It had a blue hull with a white accent stripe. It had an eight inch draft, with the centerboard out, and three feet with it down. Also, both the centerboard and mahogany rudder could kick up and out.

One person could rig the 23 foot mast, with jib and mainsail, totaling 135 square feet. It has three storage lockers and flotation built in. It seats four, if they know how to sail, and two under any circumstances. It has a 10-hp Evinrude outboard motor on the stern, just in case.

I am a fair-weather sailor, although I do like to run with the wind on occasion. However, my sailing skills paled in comparison to those of others I'd read about. I recently read a news story about a 16-year-old school girl from Australia who sailed alone and unassisted around the world. She set sail in October, and sailed for 210 days. Her trip covered almost 23,000 nautical miles, as she traveled north-east through the South Pacific and across the equator, then south to Cape Horn, at the tip of South America, then across the Atlantic Ocean to

South Africa, and then through the Indian Ocean and around southern Australia. During her months at sea, she struggled against homesickness, loneliness, and boredom. She also battled wild storms, and on one occasion her mast was pushed 180 degrees into the water. On the Tuesday after her safe return, she turned 17 and was just old enough to get her driver's license. Amazing.

We all wonder on occasion just how brave we are. However, very few of us are willing to create an opportunity to actually test our courage against formidable odds. We prefer to play it safe and wonder, *what if.*

Inverness was a charming village located twenty-four miles west of Petaluma. The village consisted of Mary's General Store, Seth's Market, Vladimir's Restaurant, Ma Dodge's Café, and a Chevron gas station and tire repair shop. Travelers went through it on their way to the Point Reyes Light House and the surrounding ocean beaches. To the south was Bear Valley Ranch, now a part of the Point Reyes National Sea Shore Preserve.

Hat had arranged for me to store my boat at Tod Lassen's boathouse; it was the only one there for public use. The boathouse was as old as the village. It was a small boat-house erected over a narrow wharf that extended thirty feet out into Tomales Bay. There was a sign *Boats for Hire* in big bold, but fading white paint, on the outside wall. I was sure that the sign had been there for years. I never questioned why no one else ever used the facilities there.

My boat was resting on two large fiber slings that were attached to a motorized winch, which lifted the boat with me in it, swung it out over the water, and set it down alongside the floating dock. One side of the sling automatically detached and dropped under the boat when the tension slacked. I then paddled it the few feet to the dock, tied it up, then returned the slings and winch inside the boathouse.

I left the boathouse and drove the few hundred yards back to the edge of town, then turned right and drove up the short switchback streets to the mesa, and veered left past the elementary school, to where the street dead-ended in front of Hat's garage.

Hat's house was a shingle-covered cottage built in the 1920s. Several pine trees loomed over the roof and yard, and the yard was thick with broom. It seemed dark except for the walkway from the garage to the house. The walkway was trimmed with large sea shells and drift wood that Hat had collected. There was a stack of firewood nestled between two pine trees alongside the house, in preparation for winter,

As, until recently, a wood stove was Hat's only source of heat during the winter.

"Matthew, my boy," said Hatfield, as he came out to greet me. "Come in. Let me show you my new toy."

The entry door led though a small porch, into a roomy but crude kitchen and then into a huge great room; a combination dining room, family room, and living room, with the fire place and stone hearth at one end. Coiled pipes were at the rear of the fireplace, and water ran from the intake source through the pipes and to the hot water storage tank. That was a common way to get hot water in cottages that originally did not have electricity. However, Hat had the house completely wired, and included a 50-gallon electric water heater, shortly after he moved in.

The walls and ceiling were of light mahogany, and two kerosene lanterns hung from ceiling hooks. They originally were the main source of light for the house, but were now used only when the power went out. Two good sized bedrooms were off of the great room. A full bath was off of the front bedroom, and a toilet was located just off of the rear entry porch.

Hat gave me the grand tour because I had not seen the house since he had recently remodeled the interior.

"Hat, I don't see many changes from the last time I was here."

"Voila, mon centre informatique!! Just look at my new computer center." And indeed, he had installed a new desk in one corner of the great room, and he had the latest and largest HP computer, with a 24-inch flat-screen monitor, and a HP laser color printer, fax, copier combination, as his new toy. He had a double-paned window installed in the corner walls that extended four feet in either direction from the corner, and was four feet high.

"Nice, Hat. Now you can play like the rest of the kids."

"Remember, Matthew, men only grow up on the outside," and he deliberately gave out a boyish grin.

"I see you finally have a view of the back yard and path that leads down to the tennis court and to the street to town."

"Yes, Matthew, although no one ever walks up to this end of the path except me. But, if they ever did, I would see them."

"Hat, you never told me why you settled here in Inverness and in an old cottage like this one."

"I didn't just settle here, Matthew. I guess I was so interested in your childhood and growing up that I didn't tell you anything about mine. You see, my grandfather was a successful cattle and feed rancher around the Fernley and Lovelock areas, and he also had a successful gold mine in the hills south of Winnemucca. He could afford to hire hands to work the ranches and mine, so he and my grandmother could travel. He found this little jewel of a village, with its cool morning and evening climate, that allowed them to beat the Nevada summer heat. He had this cottage built for their summer retreats. I traced the records and found that it cost him $2,700 to have it built."

"This was your grandparents cottage," a statement that I said almost like a question.

"Yes, and I spent many wonderful summers here as a boy during the 1940's. My favorite time was the Fourth of July. They detoured traffic around the main street, to behind the store areas, and they held races down the main street in front of Mary's store: three-legged races, potato races, granddad's and grandma's races, a sailor's race, a soldier's race, and many races for the kids. Bill Eastward would call the races. I was a fast runner as a 10-year old, and once won a race. Later, in the morning, we would adjourn to the tennis court and watch Bill and Hank someone play a hard game of singles. Ah, what a time, Matthew, what a time."

"So how did you end up with it, Hat?"

"Well, my father and grandfather never got along, so the house went to my uncle when my grandparents died, and I was never invited back again. However, my uncle's line died out after one generation, and I was able to buy the cottage in an estate sale in 1995. I vacationed here from time to time, and then moved here in 2000, after settling all my affairs in Nevada."

"Just out of curiosity, Hat, what did it cost you to buy it?" I thought Hat was in such a mood to share that he would answer without remembering how closed-mouth he is.

"Would you believe $375,000?"

"Yikes," I blurted.

"Well, it just happened to be when prices were at their highest, and any property in this village was very expensive. It's still worth that much, or more, even though the housing market is in a slide in most areas. Not here! And besides, Matthew, that was about half a year's income from my Nevada gold mine, which is still producing well."

"You old fox, Hat. I've got to hand it to you. You're living life on the high end and on your terms."

"Why Matthew, I wouldn't have it any other way." He winked and beamed with satisfaction. "Say, we had better be on our way. We'll can catch the incoming tide."

Chapter 35

Hat had packed our lunch: sandwiches of chopped beef mixed with mayonnaise, green bell peppers, and onions, and prepared a home-made red skinned potato salad. This he had complimented with our choice of *Pellegrini* old clone Zinfandel or Scaggs Vineyard Napa Valley Mt. Veeder Montage, which Boz Scaggs described as a blend of classic southern Rhone varietals: mourvedre, grenache , syrah and counoise. What a feast it would be.

We set off from the boathouse dock and tacked our way slowly northwest toward the mouth. Tomales Bay is actually a large estuary of approximately 164,000 acres, located about 40 miles north of San Francisco. The mouth opens into Bodega Bay, and the mouth is especially dangerous, I am told, with high swells and a strong current. I always stayed away from the mouth and monitored the tides carefully, so that I wouldn't be trying to come back in when the tide was going out.

As we passed the various coves along the southern shoreline, Hat pointed out the beaches he knew from his youth: the Chicken Ranch, which was a good place to swim, but required the bather to wear some sort of foot protection to avoid the sharp oyster shells that covered the bottom of the cove; Teacher's Beach, which was a better place to swim because it didn't have any shells; and Shell Beach, which was misnamed because it didn't have any shells either, and was a great place to swim, although an occasional jellyfish might come by and sting the swimmer.

We arrived at Hog's Island, located about four miles south of the mouth of the Bay. It was a 2-acre island that had been privately owned by a number of individuals from 1885 until 1996, when it became a part of the Point Reyes National Seashore. The island is now uninhabited, but remains of a structure and a small pier show evidence of prior human habitation. The island is a pupping ground for Harbor Seals, so access is restricted during pupping season. Fortunately, it wasn't pupping season.

I lowered the sails and pulled up the center board just as we hit the beach. I got out and pulled the boat farther up onto the beach so that Hat could get out without getting wet. He handed me the cooler, and we found a large flat rock and a make-shift table that someone had made out of drift wood. I set our cooler down, took out the wine, and poured a large glass of Zin for me and one of the Montage for Hat.

There was only a slight breeze today, for which we were thankful because the winds can come up quickly and make this an unpleasant place to be. We passed the lunch time in light conversation, and Hat added more memories of his childhood times at Inverness and the coastal beaches.

After lunch, and another glass of wine, Hat turned to me with a serious expression on his face. "Matthew, I want to tell you a story which might or might not be related to what you are doing in Sacramento. You know that I enjoy doing research on the computer and probing my nose in the business of politics."

"Sure Hat. That's your red wagon," citing a line from a Bob Wills song with which I knew Hat was familiar.

"Well, I also belong to a group, a society, a secret society, a world-wide society of others like me who research into politics, and are always looking for ways to set things right with the world. Recently, we have pooled a lot of information and have developed several scenarios about the presidential election four years from now. Mind you, these are hypothetical scenarios, based on selected information. Nevertheless, your man, Adair Zandi keeps coming up. He seems to be connected to a minority political party, if you will, in Iran, and rumor has it that somehow he hopes to overthrow the current administration in Iran and take over the country. It is rich in oil reserves and has a strategic location for power in the Middle East."

"Hat, you're going beyond me. How is this connected to what I am doing?" I poured another glass of wine for each of us.

"This man, Zandi and the Committee are connected, and have been quietly lobbying to have our current administration find a way to have our military attack Iran and oust the ruling party. They are using the threat of Iran having nuclear weapons as a ruse to make their cause a worthy and popular one. Our current outgoing president is too dense to recognize the potential, and can think only of sitting under a tree at his ranch and sipping whiskey. He longs to get back to that bottle. The vice-president, though eager, lacks the authority. The newly elected president will not be a man easily duped into a foolish invasion of Iran, so the Committee and Zandi will lie low. Their plan seems to be to wait until the next election, four years from now, because by then the voting public will have grown impatient with the man in office."

Hat took a drink of his wine and continued, "The thought is that the president's party will lose control of the House in the next election and the new House will then proceed to undermine the President's every effort, from defunding his health, withdraw troops from Iraq, and to sending them into Afghanistan.

He will also be blamed for the economy not recovering from the recession created by the mortgage debacle. In the next election this opposing party will counter him by putting forth Alicia Lincoln, the most influential woman in politics today, as president, and your Governor Osborne as vice president. You might not be aware of it, Matthew, but the Committee has unofficially formed a radical splinter group of the opposing party, currently known as the Boston Revolt Party, and it is growing in strength across the nation. Their cries will exaggerate the President's failures and stress the reactionary solutions. That group will support Osborne, while the mainstream party folks will support Alicia Lincoln."

"Hat, we both know that Alicia Lincoln is too wise to be fooled into attacking Iran. She'll open negotiations with them and work through diplomacy, not force, just like our newly elected president would like to do. And besides, what about the current vice-president? Won't he expect to be the party's candidate in four years?"

"Not a chance. He's too old and will have put his foot in his mouth a sufficient number of times over the next four years to share in the President's discredit. Now listen to this: if Alicia Lincoln is assassinated by an Iranian, after her election, possibly as she attempts to fly into Iran or engage in negotiations, Osborne would take over the government. He, my dear Matthew, will do what those who put him in power tell him to do. Enter Zandi and the Committee."

"Hat, this all sounds too wild a theory to be plausible. And how does this fit in with what I'm doing in Sacramento?"

"As I said, this is only one scenario our group has developed, but it is the only one that connects all the information we have collected. We want to watch Governor Osborne and any of his staff, including Ms. Reed-Wilder, to see what role they play in allotting or getting these corrections funds from the federal government. We think that the Committee might have fronted the money to a few individuals who are in line to receive the corrections grants, such as Robbins, and one that you won't ever see who, in a sense, is your counterpart in southern California, working with the local sheriffs' departments.

"Who is he, Hat, the one in southern California?"

"His name is John Natalie, younger son of Gaetano Natalie, a familiar name to us both. He is well organized and looks to be a cinch to administer the corrections funding for eight community centers within the Los Angeles basin, and two in San Diego, in cooperation with the local sheriffs' departments."

"Hat, I am overwhelmed by you. I think that you know more than I do about what I'm doing. How did you get so involved in all this research and scenario gaming?"

"Well Matthew, my group and I have been collecting information about both the Committee's work in Washington and Adair Zandi, and when you explained what you are doing, it all seemed to fall into place, at least as far and the corrections funding and Osborne go. We'll just bide our time and watch the machinations that occur."

"It sounds as though you are hoping to watch a gathering storm."

"We'll wait and see, Matthew, and I'll keep you informed of anything that might affect you or your work. Otherwise, we will continue dealing with theories and scenarios, and see where they take us. I must say, that I find this all very stimulating, mentally."

"I'll bet you do, Hat. This is right up your alley. However, it all seems so theoretical, and if I can borrow a phrase from Robert M. Persig's book, *Zen and the Art of Motorcycle Maintenance*, 'In the high country of the mind, one must get used to the thin air of uncertainty.' This entire situation is full of uncertainty, so keep your mind as open as your ears."

Chapter 36

We sailed back to Inverness, catching the incoming tide just right, and put my boat away in Tod Lassen's boathouse. I took Hat home. On the way, I had filled him in on what we were planning to do, and what might happen as a result. In doing so, I became aware that I too was creating scenarios, the outcome of which I knew not.

Hat seemed disturbed that we were going to intervene with Robbins. He would have preferred to let the drama play itself out to its own end. He could afford to feel that way because he was an observer, not a player, and had the luxury of enjoyment without involvement.

Early that evening, I pulled into my driveway at home and noticed that the lights were on in my house and in Perry's house as well, which meant that they were home from cooking class. I wondered what they might be up to now.

Libby met me at the door and gave me a quick surprise kiss on the mouth, smiled, and walked quickly through the living room and into the kitchen.

"Zee, I didn't know if or when you would be home so I didn't prepare any dinner. Are you hungry?"

"What, no French cuisine ready for a hungry man home from work?" I offered in jest.

"I'll tell you Zee, Perry and I cooked so many kinds of foods with a French flavor that I am burned out. I might eat something, but I want something light and plain."

"Libby, how about we go back to the basics, you know, our Sunday night tomato soup and grilled cheese sandwiches?"

Libby broke into a wide smile. She beamed, as though I had said something that unlocked her special warmth; a certain presence she exuded, and that she and I shared so long ago. I felt it draw me in, and I smiled as well.

We ate our tomato soup and grilled cheese sandwiches slowly, making small talk as we did. I told her about what a fine sail Hat and I had, *sans* the serious conversation. She told me about her cooking classes and how much Perry seemed to enjoy being out.

After we finished eating, I did the few dishes, stretched, and walked into the living room. I didn't have anything but wine to drink because I didn't want to tempt Libby.

I noticed that the house was clean and neat, that the furniture had not been rearranged and the same old curtains hung inside the windows. They did look as if they had been washed, however.

"I'm off to bed early, Libby. I have to be in Sacramento by 8:00 in the morning."

"Oh, Zee, I was hoping we would have a few days together."

"Sorry Libby. Duty calls. However, if all goes well, I'll wrap this job up sooner than I thought. Either way, I'll come back soon, and spend that time."

She smiled and was accepting, without showing the resentment I was used to from her in similar situations in the past. *But that was the past.*

Chapter 37

I arrived at the BOC office shortly after 8:00 a.m. Thankfully, the Dragon Lady was not in as yet, so I was free to collect my thoughts and papers. A quick phone call to Orneles confirmed that the stage was set.

At about 8:30, I put Robbins' file in my briefcase, patted my shoulder holster and shoved my Colt .380 in its waist band holster, and left my office. Jill was on the phone as I passed her counter, and left the building.

I gave the routine pencil-under-the-hood check, started the car and headed east on Capitol Avenue, which becomes Folsom Boulevard about five miles out. It was already hot out, and a wind was coming up from the south. It usually doesn't get windy until the afternoon. I hoped this wasn't an omen.

It suddenly occurred to me that in all the excitement, I had forgotten to notify AAA of my truck loss. Today, for sure. I missed my pickup truck, but the air-conditioning on this Buick already offered a nice buffer against the valley heat.

I drove right up to the door of the motel office and parked. I didn't want to leave any opportunity for anyone to see me as I forced Robbins to leave. I walked to the room that Robbins had converted into his office and knocked. He opened the door. He was smiling and acting cocky, as usual. I don't think he suspected anything.

"Come on in, Dr. Worth. Sit down. What's this about changing the evaluation component?" He sat behind his desk and gestured to a chair across from him. He looked the same as I remembered, flowered shirt, Wrangler jeans, and snake skin boots. His white Stetson hat hung from a wall hook above his desk.

"Here, let me show you, Bob." I opened my briefcase, placed his file on his desk before him, and walked around his desk to stand behind him. I leaned over his right shoulder and flipped two pages in his file and pointed. As soon as his full attention was on the file, I drew my .357 revolver and shoved the barrel against his neck just below his right ear. He froze his movements, but spoke.

"What the hell do you think you're doing?"

I shoved the barrel harder into his neck. "I'm sorry to tell you this, Bob, but I'm onto your little scam, and you're all through."

"What! You a fucking cop, Worth? You think you're going to bust me for something. You got another thought coming."

"No, Robbins. I'm no cop. It's just that I like your action here, and I'm taking it. You're out."

"Fuck you, Worth. You get nothing. You're not dealing with some two bit punk here, you know."

"I know. That's why you're out. I made a deal with your bosses. I take you out, and they replace you with someone who isn't greedy and will do as he is told. I control the funds to be certain that they all go to programs that we front. I get a piece of the action, and you get dead." I shoved the gun into his right ear.

He was starting to sweat, and I could see his hands and feet moving ever so slightly, preparing to turn and jump me, if he decided he could.

"Don't even think about it. I'd just as soon shoot you here as anywhere."

"Listen, Worth You got me all wrong. They got me wrong. I can be reasonable. Let's talk about this."

"I'll tell you, Robbins, you have three choices: one, you can attempt to jump me now, and I blow a large hole under your ear; or two, you can ride out somewhere with me now to an isolated spot, and I blow a large hole under your ear; or, three, you can ride with me into town and speak with your bosses. If you can convince them that you're indispensable, you live. Anyway you play it, I'm in. Which way do you want it?"

"You don't give a guy much choice."

"I don't intend to."

"O.K. Worth, you're in, but where or how I don't know."

"Well, I know how I'm in, so let's go into town and see if you're still in."

"O.K. Worth. No need for the gun," and he started to rise from the chair.

I shoved the gun barrel into his ear again. "I'll tell you when you can move." I pulled a short bungee cord from my pocket, clipped one hook on the front of the trigger guard and pulled it around his face.

"Open your mouth." He did, and I pulled the cord into the opening, wrapped it around the other side of his face, and secured the second hook in the front trigger guard.

"Now, that way you'll stay within easy reach. We're going to walk outside and get into your car. You're going to drive. If you run, I shoot. If anyone tries to stop us, I shoot. Understand?"

He didn't say a word. I got him out of the chair and we walked outside. His pink Lincoln, with the steer horn hood ornament, was parked in a space thirty feet away. There was no one in sight. I pointed toward the car, and we walked together. We had about ten feet to go, when a motel room door opened, and Monroe came stalking out.

I spun us both around to face him. "Get back in the room, Monroe. Your boss and I are going for a ride." He kept walking slowly toward us.

"You want me to get him, boss?"

Robbins hesitated, trying to figure which way to go. Monroe hesitated, trying to decide if he could get at me soon enough. I couldn't allow them any more time to think. I was holding the .357 in my left hand. I cross-drew the .380 with my right hand, and pointed it at Monroe. "If you are not back inside that room by the time I say three, you big dumb ox, you won't have the opportunity to get anyone ever again. One....two...." I leveled the gun and sighted. He turned and ran back to the room and slammed the door.

While I was counting I couldn't help but recall what Orneles had said about Monroe at our meeting the other night, 'Shoot the son-of-a-bitch. It will only add a touch of sincerity to your intentions toward Robbins.' I wanted to.
I almost did.

I returned the Colt to its pants belt holster, and Robbins and I entered the car through the passenger side door. As he drove away, I turned the .357 sideways and lowered it to rest on his shoulder No need to arouse the curiosity of other motorists. We proceeded west on Folsom Boulevard to Power Inn Road, but he balked when I told him to turn left.

"Hey, Worth, I thought we had a deal. You were gonna let me talk to them."

"You're going to talk to them, don't worry. Turn left."

He did, but he started to sweat again, and his right cheek began to twitch. Then, I noticed him glancing into his rear view mirror. After the third glance, his twitching stopped, and a sly smile spread across his face. I turned and looked behind us. The police cruiser was coming fast, lights and siren on. Robbins pulled over and so did the police car.

"Christ," I tried to sound convincing. Quickly, I unhooked the bungee cord from the trigger guard, shoved the gun into my shoulder holster, and yanked the cord out of Robbins' mouth. You better play it straight, Robbins, or I'll take you out for good."

"Hey, don't worry. We're partners now, ain't we?" He stopped, turned off the engine, and let his hands rest on top of the steering wheel.

One officer approached Robbins and asked for his license and registration. I could see the other officer moving up on my side. Suddenly, the first officer pulled out his service gun and thrust it through the open window, pointing it at my mid-section. It was a Smith and Wesson .40-cal.

semi-automatic, and the officer was holding it right in front of Robbins' face. I could imagine Robbins hoping that the officer wouldn't shoot. He gulped, and stared cross-eyed at the barrel.

"I'm only going to tell you this once, mister." The officer was speaking to me in a commanding tone. "Keep your hands in sight, open your door slowly, step out, turn around, and place your arms on the roof of the car. My partner is there and he wants to talk to you."

I exited the car, turned around, and laid my arms on the car roof. Officer Pettigrew, his nameplate read, was standing there with his gun drawn.

"Mister, when we were coming up behind you back there it looked like you were holding a gun on this man, and then you pulled it away and stashed it somewhere. You got a gun on you now, mister?"

"Yes, in a shoulder holster, but I can explain."

Officer Pettigrew gingerly pulled back the lapel of my coat and removed my .357 revolver. "Put your hands behind your head, sir." Then, he handcuffed me.

The other officer stood up and spoke to Pettigrew. "The driver is Bob Robbins, a state parole agent. His ID checks. Says this guy pulled a gun on him, and was making him drive somewhere out in the country to rob him. Says he'll come down to the station, give us the details, and request a complaint. Put that guy in the car; we'll book him."

By the time Pettigrew had me secured in the back seat of the police cruiser, Robbins had made a U-turn and headed back toward Folsom Boulevard. I watched his car to the corner, where he turned left toward town. I didn't see Orneles, but what looked like an undercover car went roaring by. I don't know why they call them undercover cars. Most of them are so conspicuous that anyone could spot them.

I didn't see any other cars, but I knew that Orneles and his men were in radio contact. I had a radio scanner in my briefcase so that I could at least hear what was happening. At the end of the tail, Orneles was going to give a location over the radio for us to meet. He had no way to confirm that I heard, but he had to assume I would be back in my car by that time.

Both officers got into the police car, with Swift driving, and we continued going south on Power Inn Road.

"Say, fellows. My car is in the other direction." Neither officer acknowledged that they heard me.

Pettigrew had taken my .357, but had not bothered to pat me down. The Colt was still in my waist band holster. I didn't think anything about it at the time because it wasn't a real arrest. With my hands cuffed behind me, I couldn't quite reach it. I never realized before how uncomfortable it was to ride in the back seat of a police car, with handcuffs on. When I was young and supple, I could bring my cuffed hands down and over my feet, so they would be in front. Now, my body parts wouldn't move in the right directions to allow that.

"Hey, Pettigrew. Enough is enough. I need to get back to my car."

Pettigrew turned around and spoke through the protective grill work. "We're supposed to book you. We can't do that if we take you back to your car." They both laughed.

"We're driving in the wrong direction, both for you to book me and to take me back to my car. Turn around," I commanded. "Didn't Orneles explain that as soon as the driver of the other car left, you were to drive me to my car?"

"Orneles didn't say anything about doing that. In fact, he said we were to drive out to Hutchinson's abandon quarry, put a bullet in your head, and concrete on your feet, and drop you into the flooded quarry diggings." I froze. That son-of-a-bitch. *He set me up, and he's probably going to hit MacClanahan too. No one but us three knew all the information. He must have made up that story about meeting with Holden. He'll be in the clear and the conspiracy can continue.*

I reached my hands around my left side as far as I could, but I could not quite reach my gun. My fingertips just scratched the holster. I moved my body sideways, as if to sit on the floor, and pushed the holster down on the car seat, trying to force it up and out of my waistband. The holster was snapped securely and wouldn't move, but I could feel the gun loosen and slip out onto the seat. I moved back into a sitting position, grabbing the Colt in my right hand as I did. *Now what?*

Pettigrew turned and eyed me, then Swift pulled the car off the road and stopped. They both turned and stared at me with deadpan expressions.

"Looks a little white, don't he Jim," Swift said.

"Sure does, Swifty. We must have scared him. Hope he didn't shit his pants."

"Assholes," I said. It felt good to use the police officer's favorite descriptive pronoun and direct it to them. When an officer uses the term *asshole*, he is referring to anyone who does not agree with his definition of the situation. I gave it the same meaning.

Swift and Pettigrew stared at each other momentarily, and then looked back at me. Then, they burst out laughing at the same time, and carried on laughing and slapping their legs until they were beet-red in the face.

"*Gotcha,*" said Pettigrew, pointing his finger at me. Swift made a quick U-turn and raced back down Power Inn Road, with lights flashing and siren blaring. He had reached Folsom Boulevard and turned right before their joke sunk in.

"You guys are real funny." I tried not to show too much irritation, even though I didn't appreciate their brand of humor. I'll wait until I get out of this car and these cuffs.

"Orneles didn't fill us in on the details of this deal, but it didn't seem like anything big. We thought we might as well have a little fun in the process."

Pettigrew wasn't apologetic. In fact, he made it sound as if they deserved to satisfy their whim at my pleasure.

I didn't say anything more except to direct them back to my car. On the way, I managed to raise my coat and shove the Colt back into my waistband. Swift parked behind my car and Pettigrew got out, opened my door, removed the cuffs, and returned my revolver. "No harm done, huh?"

I put the .357 back in its shoulder holster. "I'll tell you fellas, I hope I never run into you again. Orneles might think you're O.K., a couple of good old boys, but I think you are two of the biggest, dumbest assholes I've ever met. We're right in the middle of a serious investigation, which you might have fucked up, and I had a gun pointed at both your asses back there, trying to decide which one to shoot first."

I pulled out the Colt and waved it in Pettigrew's face. His mouth dropped open. "I probably would have shot you first because you're the dumbest asshole. I know you were doing Orneles a favor, but next time, just do as you are asked, and don't get your kicks at someone else's expense."

I turned, and walked to my car and drove away, feeling so good inside at having told them off. It was probably the only time in my life that I would get to talk to a police officer like that, and get away with it.

Chapter 38

The traffic was light driving down Folsom Boulevard. I had preset a police scanner Orneles had given me with the frequency he would use, and I turned it on just in time to hear Orneles direct one of his men, Casey, to stop Robbins immediately, and detain him. Orneles said he was only about twelve blocks away, and that Casey should wait until Orneles arrived before attempting an arrest.

"Roger, boss," Casey replied. I have my red light on and he is pulling over to the curb now. I'll just stall him until you get here. Huh...there's a car parking behind me. Some big Black guy is getting out and walking toward my window. I'll just get rid of him first before I..." The radio transmission stopped.

I found myself yelling into the scanner, "It's Monroe. Look out, it's Monroe," but of course no sound was transmitted. I realized that Monroe had followed me with Robbins, then followed either Robbins or Orneles, and now had Casey. I floored the accelerator and, in the absence of lights and siren, put my headlights on high beam, jammed my hand down on the horn, and raced down the middle of the street. I ran four red lights, and caused one minor accident, but managed to reach the location, Casey had given, within ten minutes.

The street was blocked off at either end by police cars, and police were everywhere, stringing up their yellow 'keep-out' tape. An ambulance was idling in the middle of the block.

I parked on the side street, jumped from the car before it came to a complete stop, ducked under the yellow crime scene tape, and ran toward the ambulance. Three officers stopped me halfway there, but fortunately Orneles saw me and came right over.

"How is your man, Casey?"

"Dead. His neck has been broken. His seat belt was still buckled. He didn't have a chance."

"Damn! I heard him on my scanner say that a big Black guy was approaching his car. It must have been Monroe."

"That's what I thought, too. I put an all-points bulletin out on both Monroe and Robbins. They must be driving Monroe's car, because Robbins' Lincoln is parked over there." He pointed to the curb beyond the ambulance. "And another thing, Casey's gun is missing; a Glock 9 mm."

"Things are coming apart at the seams," I said. "It's not going to work out nice and neat the way Holden wants."

"No way to stop it now. Robbins is either after you or his co-conspirators, who he thinks set him up with you. We've got to get Robbins quick, or the entire case is going to slip right out of our fingers."

"I have another idea, Bob. Give me your pager number. Here, write it on the back of one of my cards." He did. "I'm going back to the BOC and confront the Dragon Lady. Tell her I want in now or she's out, and force her to take me to the others. I'll leave word with the receptionist where we've gone, and have her page you."

"Don't do anything rash, Matt. Maybe she's not involved at all. Then where are we?"

"I don't know Bob. I'm counting on my hunch that she's deeply involved." I turned and started to leave when I recalled that Jill didn't check out. "Shit," was the only explicative that fit the situation.

"What's wrong," Orneles asked.

"The receptionist, Jill McCloud, she didn't check out. She might be a phony. I don't know if I can trust her."

"You can trust her," said Orneles, without hesitation.

"How can you be so sure?"

"Don't ask," he replied. "You don't want to know. You can trust her, take my word for it."

I decided to take his word for it now and figure it out later. My car was hemmed in by two police cars that had arrived late, so I went over the curb, across two front lawns, and returned to the street. Three minutes later I pulled up in front of the BOC, exiting the car and cautiously entering the lobby. Jill was at her station opening the mail, one of her daily chores. She gave me a look that was half smile and half question.

"Jill," I said softly, as I approached the counter and leaned over toward her. "Has anyone come in within the last ten minutes?"

"No. Why?"

"Is the Dragon Lady here?"

"Yes. Why?"

"Never mind. Please listen carefully and do exactly as I say." I handed her my card with the pager number for Orneles on it. "I am going in to see Ms. Reed-Wilder. In a few minutes we will leave together. I'll tell you where we're going. As soon as we leave, call this number. It's a pager. When it answers, dial in your number. When a man calls you in response to your call, tell him where we've gone. He'll know what it means. Don't tell anyone else." I was giving her directions on how to call a pager as if I was telling a child. A conditioned reaction to the situation, I thought.

I opened Ms. Reed-Wilder's door, entered, and closed the door behind me. She looked up with a start.

"Dr. Worth, I'm not used to having someone walk into my office uninvited. Please leave. I'm busy."

I grabbed a straight back chair, turned it around back toward her, and straddled it, facing her.

"Dr. Worth, what is the meaning of this?" She put on the most indignant air. As I sat down, her eyes widened, stretching out the blue liner around her eyes, yielding a clownish appearance. She started to rise.

"Sit down, Ms. Reed-Wilder, or should I say Mrs. Zandi, or Mariana Natalie. We have something to discuss, you and I."

Her expression became frozen in time, and her body was suspended a few inches off her chair.

"You look surprised, Mariana. Oh, may I call you Mariana?" I was unable to keep the sarcasm and pleasure from my voice. "Did you folks think you were going to just waltz right in and dance away with all those millions?"

"What do you want?" Her tone was sharp and cold now, and she had seated herself and folded her hands tightly on the desk in front of her.

"I want in. I'm your new partner," I demanded.

"We don't have partners. Who are you and what do you know?"

"Me, I'm just a hard working consultant who happened to figure out your little scheme. Soon, I'm going to be a rich consultant."

"What do you know? Who sent you here?" she asked in that same demanding tone. She was staring me eye to eye, and in her expression was a mixture of hate and terror.

"I know that you and you ex-husband, Adair Zandi came out from New York a few years ago, and founded your Committee to win elections and bribe politicians. Somehow, you learned about the corrections grant money and placed your yes-man in the Governor's office to help you get it."

I hadn't meant to mention Governor Osborne because I wasn't sure he was the one. I had intended to bluff her into naming her partners, and his name just came out. Perhaps because in the back of my mind, I was sure. Anyway, I had to play this out the way I started .

"How did you find out?"

"Robbins told me."

"Robbins?" She was startled at first, and then re-gained her composure. "He never would. He may not be too bright, but he's not that stupid."

She acted as if she had the upper hand. Time for some better lies. "He didn't have a choice, actually. You see, I sat him and Monroe down on a bed in that motel of his and demanded a piece of his action, in return for recommending approval of his proposal. I didn't know about you at the time. Well, Robbins objected to me leaning on him, and refused. So I just took out my trusty revolver."

I took out my .357 and pointed it at her without aiming. "I put the gun to Monroe's head and blew his brains all over the wall of that motel room. After that, Robbins was much more cooperative, and told me the whole story."

"That bastard." she snarled. "That wimpy little bastard. Where is Robbins now?"

"Well, I hate to tell you Mariana, but I left him back at the motel, splattered all over the wall alongside Monroe." I hefted my gun twice in my hand. "I didn't think we needed him anymore."

"You're a real fool, Worth. The guy was a creep, but the cons trusted him and he knew how to handle them. That's the only reason we had him in the first place."

"Not to worry," I acted completely self-assured. " I have a man we can slip right into Robbins place without a hitch, a con himself. And, he'll work for wages, not a percentage."

I could see she was thinking about the advantages. The corners of her mouth cracked into a slight smile. "I can't say anything without consulting the others."

"I realize that, Mariana, that's why I came in here. That's what we're going to do now."

"What? Where?" She looked worried again.

"We are going to consult with the others."

"What do you mean?"

"I mean my dear Ms. Natalie, that you and I are going over to the Governor's office now and explain the situation, then we'll have him call your other partners with new arrangements, and then we'll all be friends."

"We can't do that. I'll call Adair. He will know what to do." She reached for the phone and lifted the receiver. I got up, quickly moved to her side, pushed her hand back down on the phone, and placed the barrel of my revolver in her ear.

"I'm not here asking, Mariana, I'm telling. You and I are going to see the Governor now. He's expecting us."

She jerked her head away from my gun and looked up as if in shock. "And, remember, Mariana, at this point, we really don't need you either." I touched her in the ear again with the gun barrel to emphasize my warning, then put the gun away and sat on the corner of her desk.

What a bluff; but it's working. And, I knew by now that the Governor was in on it.

"Better get your purse, Mariana." She hesitated and looked around the room quickly, like a trapped mouse looking for a way to escape the cat. Then, she opened the desk drawer and took out her purse and stood. "Let's go."

She moved with me to the door. I opened it and stepped out ahead of her. She followed part way out, and then stopped. "My medicine. I forgot it."

She returned to her desk, opened the top drawer and took out a bottle of pills, and tossed them in her purse.

I approached the counter and told Jill to phone the Governor. Tell him that we are on our way over and must have an emergency meeting right away. Then, call that pager number.

Jill nodded, and we walked out the door. So far, so good. Now, if the Governor co-operates, Orneles finds me, and Robbins doesn't, we might wrap up this case and dump it in Holden's lap. Of course, the players won't fall for the big time federal raps that he wants, but conspiracy, fraud and double murder will do for starters.

Chapter 39

I parked near the capitol building and we walked inside and stood by the elevator doors, waiting for it to descend from the third floor, where the private offices are. When the elevator came, we were the only two to get in. I pushed the 3rd floor button, the door closed, and we began our assent.

Mariana Natalie hadn't uttered a word since we left her office. I could see by her expression that she was preoccupied, the wheels were spinning a mile-a-minute, undoubtedly scheming to get ahead of me on this, and re-gain control.

The elevator door opened. No one was in the hall. We walked to the end of the corridor and around the corner to the Governor's outer office. I opened the door slowly, hoping to be ready for any trouble that might be inside. The outer office was empty. I walked across the room, bringing Mariana with me by the arm, and knocked on the inner door. It opened a few inches and the Governor peeked out, with a cautious expression. He looked back and forth, first at Mariana, then at me, as if he didn't know what else to do. I pushed open the door and led Mariana inside. I shut the door and moved slightly to the left.

Mariana looked at me, then at the Governor. "This is Dr. Worth, the federal program evaluator I told you about."

"Yes?" His voice was questioning and tentative.

"He knows, and he wants in."

Governor Osborne looked as though he had been shot. He put his hands to his face and fell back a few paces, coming to rest against his desk.

"You fool, bringing him here," blurted the governor. "He couldn't know unless you told him. Don't you realize what he's done?"

"He found out from Robbins by threatening to kill him, and then, after Robbins told him everything, he shot him. He knows the whole thing. He wants in."

"Robbins didn't tell him anything, and he isn't dead."

"What do you mean?" She had that worried look again.

"I said Robbins isn't dead. He called me just a few minutes ago from your office. He went there looking for you, claiming that we promised to cut Worth in if Worth would kill him. He knows you and Worth are coming here, but he doesn't know who is lying, you, me, or Worth. He's on his way here now to find out."

Mariana stood there in the middle of the room listening to what Osborne was saying, but the meaning didn't sink in.

"Don't you see what he's done?" Osborne repeated himself, pointing to me. "He didn't know anything. He bluffed both you and Robbins and you both fell for it. Don't you see what you've done?"

Slowly, as Osborne repeated his plea, Mariana realized what had happened; how I had suckered them. I grinned and shrugged my shoulders, when she finally looked over at me.

"You bastard!" she raged, and she reached her hand into her purse.

"Don't do it, Mariana. You'll never make it." I drew my revolver and aimed it at her, with both hands.

Just then, the side door to Osborne's office opened and Carla entered the room, a gun held in both hands and extended in a shooting position. Osborne looked relieved. *Damn, I thought. In my haste I had forgotten about her. I should have planned for that. Now what? How am I going to shoot her?*

Mariana's hand came out of her purse, holding a small revolver. I moved away from the door, edging to the left, so I could get a clear shot at Mariana without hitting anyone else. Just then the main door opened, and Robbins and Monroe burst in. Each held a gun. Robbins moved toward me a few paces, while Monroe moved to his right so that he could shoot me without hitting Robbins. What loyalty. Right behind them came Orneles with his gun drawn.

There we were, the six of us standing with guns drawn, waving our barrels back and forth and looking at each other with furtive eye movements, each trying to be the first one to size up the situation. Governor Osborne was clinging to the edge of his desk, looking pale and helpless.

I thought about what my FTO at the Reno PD told me the first day on the force. If you want to survive out here, be decisive. Have the first word and the last word, and control everything else in between. Take charge. I looked at Orneles. He seemed to sense what I was thinking and he gave a quick nod.

I fell on one knee, and shot Robbins four times, then turned and shot Monroe twice before he hit the floor. However, he was already dead; shot by Orneles.

I saw Mariana pointing her gun at me out of the corner of my eye, but before I could turn, three shots rang out and Mariana jerked back, and fell to the floor. I looked over and saw that it was Carla who had shot her.

The three us of looked at the bodies on the floor, then at each other and relaxed, pointing our guns to the floor. As Carla joined us in the center of the room, Governor Osborne dashed past her and through the side door, locking it from the other side. Before any of us reacted, we heard the breaking of glass, like a window being smashed out. Then we heard a muffled yell which quickly faded from hearing.

I threw my body against the door, but I bounced off. I stepped back and tired two shots into the lock, and pushed open the door. The three of us rushed into the room, but it was empty. All the glass had been smashed out of a window which looked out onto the capitol garden. Orneles walked over and peered down. Osborne lay on the cement drive three stories below.

As we walked back into the Governor's office, four State Police officers came running into the room, guns drawn. Orneles recognized the Sergeant, who seemed to be in charge and held up his hand to say "stop," and he told the Sergeant that the scene was secure. Everyone put their guns away. Orneles took the Sergeant aside and began to summarize what had occurred. One officer stood guard at the door, while another picked up the guns that lay on the floor. He also explained over a radio to someone on a floor below what had occurred, and ordered the top floor closed.

I looked over to where Carla had been standing, but she was gone. I hadn't seen her leave. I thought to look back in that side room, but Orneles turned away from the Sergeant, walked over to me and put his arm around my shoulders.

"Let's you and me get out of here. The State Police will handle things from here. I'll fill them in on all the details they need."

As he talked, he moved in such a way as to escort me out of the room, then grabbed my shoulder opposite him and gave me a side hug. "Say, we were pretty good back there." He relaxed his grip and smiled. "I think you shot Robbins right out of his boots," he chuckled, and did you see that expression on Monroe's face when I hit him? Zap! Right in the throat with the first shot. Man, it felt good to shoot that guy. That one was for Casey."

I didn't respond. I couldn't share his enthusiasm for the blood bath that just occurred. I wouldn't have wanted it to come out any other way, but I didn't have to like it.

We moved past the elevator doors and walked down the stairs. The elevator had been stopped at the second floor, and the State Police had the stairs blocked, but they let us they continue on down. Scores of reporters and on-lookers were filling in the first floor hall and the stairwell. We pushed our way through them, out the exit door, and emerged into the sunlight.

"What happens now, Bob?"

"I don't know for sure Matt, but I think it is as the

French croupier says, *Les Jeux Sont Faits*, the games are over. I'll call Holden when I get back to my office. Go back to your apartment. Matt, and please stay there. If you don't hear from me over the weekend, just lie low. I'll call you first thing Monday morning."

We shook hands. I had the feeling that it would be a long time before I saw Orneles again, if ever.

"Thanks, Man."

"It's been an experience." We walked away in different directions.

Chapter 40

By the time I arrived back at the apartment complex, Carla was gone. I was told that she had moved out without leaving a forwarding address. I phoned Orneles and MacClanahan, but all I got was answering machines. Everyone was gone for the weekend, and no one would call me back.

The media had a field day all weekend with Osborne's death, *Governor Commits Suicide Rather Than Face Scandal*, but no one knew what the scandal was about. Lt. Governor Randall J. Whitaker was sworn in as Governor, and vowed to keep the public informed. From the expression on his face, I don't think he was sorry to see Osborne go.

My name was never mentioned, neither were those of Carla, Mariana, Robbins, Monroe or Orneles. In fact, the entire shoot-out received only the briefest description, *Shots fired in the Capitol, three people hit*. The police promised to release a full statement when their investigation was complete.

The phrase *round up the usual suspects* came to mind.

The weekend was uneventful, because I had no one to discuss the case with, and Orneles had asked me to stay put. It was frustrating, not knowing about Carla, or knowing if anything had happened to Jill when Monroe and Robbins went to the BOC office on Friday. I took a long walk on Sunday, following the course on which Carla and I had jogged that first day we met. I missed her, but when I tried to imagine her face before me, all I could see were visions of Libby swirling around in my head. I realized, now, that it was Libby who I really missed.

Orneles phoned me at 7:30 a.m. on Monday to confirm that my job was over. Someone in Washington had pulled the plug and had yanked Holden's chain. He was fired this morning., and with him went the corrections funding, and the task force. It occurred to me that with Holden gone, my truck money was also gone. Oh, well, my insurance would cover most of the loss, and $67,000 for a few weeks work wasn't bad.

Orneles also said that Jill had left the BOC, and that there was no need for me to return there unless I had some personal items to recover. I didn't. Before I could ask, he told me to call MacClanahan for all the details. We said good bye, nothing more.

Chapter 41

I phoned MacClanahan, and we arranged to meet for lunch at the Coffee Tree Restaurant in Vacaville; half way home for each of us. After packing and cleaning the apartment, I drove to Vacaville, thinking about all the events that had occurred, and about what I might do for the rest of the summer. I still had the rental car, so a meeting with AAA, then a truck dealer, would be the first order of business.

MacClanahan was waiting for me in the same corner booth. He had already ordered hamburgers and Coors beer for us. Orneles had given him the details of Friday's events, so I sat quietly sipping my beer while he filled me in on what I didn't know. Carla was a FBI agent who had been working undercover for over a year, when Holden first got wind of the conspiracy. She was also there to keep close, and provide me with some semblance of protection, and Mac said that she really enjoyed her work. She had been re-assigned Friday afternoon, still undercover, but he did not know where.

Mac said that Jill was a career United States Postal Service Investigator, placed by Holden and Orneles, with Stapleton's consent, as receptionist so she could keep track of how many times each player used the mail to further their plans. That constituted mail fraud. Each time was worth a nickel, five years in prison. She also had been re-assigned, location unknown. Jessup had taken a long vacation. All was well.

MacClanahan said that Stapleton was re-appointed to the BOC by incoming Governor Whitaker, but that as of now the state would be taking over the correctional center programs rather than continuing to try privatization. He said that nothing further would appear in the media about any of this, and that I should forget what I knew. It was a request, not a threat, and I agreed.

I realized now that there had been several conspiracies operating at different levels during these past two weeks, and that I had been duped by all of them, including Carla and Jill. Carla's advances were just a part of the game. The con was on me. All of them knew of the setup, except me. I had been used to scare out the rats while the others waited off stage to close the curtain.

I was reflected on how difficult it is to tell what is real and what is pretense in the relationships between people. *I will be more cautious in the future. But I've said that before.*

I looked at MacClanahan. He had that familiar wry smile on his face. We shook hands.

"See ya' around, Matt."

"You take care, Mac," I replied.

Chapter 42

I phoned Libby to tell her that my job was over, and that I was on my way home. The drive home took about an hour. On the way, I tried to assess what had occurred over the past two weeks. Five dead bodies; the state's efforts to solve the prison overcrowding through privatization had been stopped before it had a chance to get started; a political scandal had been covered up; and any links to the Committee and those who controlled it had been disconnected. Adair Zandi was nowhere to be found. We were back to ground zero.

Hat might be happy that the political intrigues he and his group had been following could still be alive and well.

What had been accomplished? I wasn't sure. The entire two weeks had been a con; an exercise in folly, as Libby would later say.

On the other hand, some of the players in the Committee's scheme had been eliminated, and by insisting on my entire salary up front, I was $67,000 to the good. For me, there had been no harm, no foul, and they had paid me well. And, when I got home, Libby might be waiting for me.

Epilogue

Libby was sitting in the porch swing when I pulled in the driveway. She was wearing her same powder blue Levi's, black cotton sweater, and black cowboy boots that she wore on the day she arrived here. This time she looked fit and healthy. She looked great.

She rose immediately as I drove in, waved, and moved toward my car. I got out quickly to meet her. She gave me her best *glad to see you* smile, and then a full body hug. I felt that flush of warmth, the same sort used to fill me with joy when we met. I was glad to be home. We kissed, and went inside.

What does the future hold, Zee? I mused. *We'll see.*

www.ingramcontent.com/pod-product-compliance
Lightning Source LLC
Chambersburg PA
CBHW072224190626
46809CB00016B/463